Through the Barbed Wire

A **Wild at Heart** Mystery

Through the Barbed Wire

Isabella Allen

BROWN BOOKS KIDS

Through the Barbed Wire

Brown Books Kids
16250 Knoll Trail Drive, Suite 205
Dallas, Texas 75248
www.BrownBooksKids.com
(972) 381-0009

A New Era in Publishing®

Publisher's Cataloging-In-Publication Data

Names: Allen, Isabella.

Title: Through the barbed wire / Isabella Allen.

Description: Dallas, Texas : Brown Books Kids, [2018] | Series: A wild at heart mystery ; [book 1] | Interest age level: 009-012. | Summary: "Homeschooled all her life, Isla's best friends are the squirrels and deer on the property, and she speaks their languages better than her own. As Isla introduces her new friend Cash to the wild places she loves so much, things on the property begin to change in dangerous ways ... Isla, with Cash's help, sets out to find the truth behind the trespassers on the property and uncovers a ruthless plot"--Provided by publisher.

Identifiers: ISBN 9781612549835

Subjects: LCSH: Nature--Juvenile fiction. | Wildfires--Juvenile fiction. | Friendship--Juvenile fiction. | Human-animal communication--Juvenile fiction. | CYAC: Nature--Fiction. | Wildfires--Fiction. | Friendship--Fiction. | Human-animal communication--Fiction. | LCGFT: Detective and mystery fiction.

Classification: LCC PS7.1.A454 Th 2018 | DDC [Fic]--dc23

ISBN 978-1-61254-983-5
LCCN 2017954564

Printed in the United States
10 9 8 7 6 5 4 3 2 1

For more information or to contact the author, please go to

www.WildAtHeartMysteries.com.

Vic, Alaina, and Preston:
if y'all hadn't encouraged me that night at Culture,
I wouldn't have written this book.

Acknowledgments

I would like to thank everyone who supported me while writing and publishing this book. Without y'all, none of this would have been possible.

First, I want to thank my dad. There is no way I could have published this book without you. I want to thank my mom for keeping a promise that she made to me when I was ten: that if I finished a book, we'd get it published. I would also like to thank my grandpa for constantly encouraging me throughout the two years I was writing this novel. I want to thank my cousin, Ella, for all of the adventures we've shared; I hope they never end. To the rest of my family, thank you for supporting me through this process.

I would like to thank Milli Brown, founder of Brown Books, for publishing my story; I still can't believe this is happening. Thank you to everyone who worked on my novel: Sherry LeVine, for taking time to meet with me and for emailing me everything I needed; Hallie Raymond, for editing this book; and Cynthia Meadows, for illustrating this book.

Thank you to all of the teachers who taught me how to write and create stories. I would especially like to thank my teacher, Mrs. Kimberly Nichols, for taking time out of her busy schedule to give me feedback on stories that weren't even assignments. And I would like to thank my teacher, Mrs. Cheryl Weaver, for answering all of my incessant questions about book publishing and making me believe that I could do it.

CHAPTER ONE

Isla sat in her favorite meadow of the prairie as she waited for the sun to peek over the distant hills. A gentle breeze blew through her long, tangled, dirty-blonde hair. She took a deep breath of the fresh spring air, sighed, and smiled. She ran her bare toes through the soft soil. A shiver ran down her spine as the excitement rose within her. Her big, bright, brown eyes watched in anticipation as the sun began to stretch over the distant hills. She jumped up to race the rays of golden sunshine. Her little feet had grown hard and accustomed to running over the prairie.

She ran up a hill just as the sun caught up with her and took in the amazing view of the meadow filling with light. A herd of white-tailed deer grazed, an owl swooped down to pick up a field mouse, and various types of birds flew through the morning sky. She knew them, every one. She had studied them day after day. Isla was only eleven, but she knew so much more than many did about the prairie and forest animals.

Isla got down on all fours and casually walked toward the deer, occasionally stopping to pretend to graze. She acted as though her interest was not in the deer but in the fresh, green grass. The deer were used to seeing her and didn't fret. She had discovered many months ago that walking directly toward them didn't work. It helped that she was small—very petite for her age, Isla was often mistaken for a nine-year-old. Soon she was walking step in step with the deer. She let out a little whine, and a doe rushed to her to see what was wrong. The mother deer couldn't help responding to any baby creature's call for help. Now this doe would act as a mother to Isla for the day. Isla loved this; it made her feel like one of them, and she never grew weary of it.

There were certain plants among the grass that were edible, and Isla munched on them to keep her satisfied. Isla stayed with the deer until noon, when the eldest buck suddenly whipped his head up and uneasily took a few steps forward. Looking back and forth through the trees and overgrown brush, he alerted the others that danger was near. Isla gulped with fear. If this was a coyote, it would be hard to keep up with the safety of the herd, and coyotes hunted deer in packs. Isla knew they wouldn't go for her, but she didn't want to witness the death of another deer. Her "mother doe" nudged Isla, pushing her to her feet, and the herd began to run. The sound of Isla's dad's old pickup truck drifted into the air. She sighed with relief, knowing that it was just him. She was able to keep up with the deer just well enough that she knew where they were headed.

The deer stopped at the creek that Isla loved to visit the most. It had wonderful, fresh water and ended in a little pool that, at its deepest, reached Isla's shoulders. It was the perfect place to cool off in the summer. There were little fish, frogs, and turtles living inside, and they were fun to watch. The deer began to drink, and Isla gladly joined them. She had gradually developed an immunity to the parasites in the water. The water was cool and refreshing, far better than what any local store had to offer.

Isla walked down to the little pool and cleaned up a bit; her father wouldn't want her coming home this filthy. Her nails were full of soil, her skin was almost brown with dirt, and her hair had all sorts of stuff in it. She did her best to clean up and brushed off her torn old blue jeans and her brown shirt, which read "Texas" in red, white, and blue. The shirt belonged to her mother and was quite big on Isla, but she didn't care. It was comfortable and made Isla feel closer to her mom.

Isla took one last look at the herd and snuck off. Watching animals sneak around had taught Isla how to do it, and the deer didn't notice. Judging by the sun, it was about 2:00 p.m. Isla found the old trail that led to the main dirt road. A few birds sang, and Isla sang out a few notes in response. Everything around her quieted as the birds listened. Then they took a turn singing a song. It was a game Isla often played with them, and she played it now until she found the dirt road and crawled through the barbed-wire fence.

Ferdinand, the family's old black lab–greyhound mix, slowly stood up to greet Isla, panting loudly, ears laid back. He had a little limp, so he walked slowly, gently wagging his tail. Isla greeted him and gave him a few pats, and he sat down on her feet and leaned against her to be pet some more. Isla scratched his favorite place on his stomach, and Ferdinand lay down, satisfied. She stepped over him and walked up the old wood steps of her porch.

Isla lived with her father on ten thousand acres in a small old white house. It needed some work, Isla knew, but they were barely in it anyway. Isla was always outside, her dad was always at work, and her mom was currently in Scotland, taking care of Isla's Grandma Ainsley, an elderly Scottish lady who was quite stubborn. Isla's mom had begged her to come to America because of her failing health, but Grandma Ainsley said again and again, "Ah wis born in this hoose, 'n' ah will die in this hoose!" Since there was no one else to care for her, Isla's mom had reluctantly left Isla and her dad to move in with Grandma Ainsley all the way in Scotland. The house felt empty now without her.

The old screen door creaked as Isla opened it. She walked into the kitchen, where her dad was reading the newspaper. His dark brown hair was especially wild today, and he had yet to unroll his sleeves from the last time he had washed his hands. His skin was already starting to darken, and it was freckling from working in the sun.

He looked above his glasses and smiled.

"You're back! Mom sent a letter, it's right on the counter over there," he said as he pointed behind him.

Isla scampered across the old, disfigured tile floor and picked up the envelope. It contained a few cool pictures of

Scotland and Grandma Ainsley. She tried her best to read the letter, but it was hard to do with dyslexia.

She paused when she heard her father mutter a few words to himself, something he often did when frustrated. "That much money for ten thousand acres? Pfft! My land's worth way more than that!" Isla sighed. Many people were always trying to buy the land. But so far, no one had offered enough money to convince her father to sell.

Isla took the pictures her mother had sent to her room. Her room was small and didn't have much in it. She had never been all that into toys as a child and didn't care for new clothes. She had her bed and her nightstand, and that was about it. Isla grabbed her Scotch tape and taped the pictures on the wall with the rest. The pictures on her wall had become a sort of timeline wallpaper. The timeline began on the edge of the wall with pictures of both sides of the family before Isla was born; then, about halfway across the wall, started pictures of baby Isla. The pictures went on through the years to Isla's second wall. The photo mural was the most amazing thing in the house, and every time family came, they went straight to her room to see it. When Isla wasn't living among the animals, she was in her room, gazing at the wall. She didn't even use her bed much. If it were up to her, she'd live outside completely. But her father would only let her spend the night outside occasionally. He knew that she wouldn't stay in a tent but would probably spend the night in an abandoned coyote den.

Ferdinand started to bark at the door. Isla walked to his food bin by the door and fetched his evening scoop of kibble. He wagged his tail and started hobbling over to his food bowl as soon as she opened the door. Ferdinand was Isla's talking buddy. She was afraid to speak around people because she had a hard time saying what she wanted to. The words just didn't fall into place like everyone else's, which was one of the reasons why she'd refused to go to school. But she knew that Ferdinand didn't care how she talked. He loved hearing her voice no matter how it came out.

She tried her best to say, "Ferdinand, they say only the strong survive, but you're living proof that they just ain't right."

She patted him, and he wagged his tail as he gulped down his food.

"You've been trucking on for twelve whole years and still love life," she said with a smile.

Ferdinand had been a happy, loyal dog for as long as Isla could remember. He had always been there for her, and she wished he always would. She left him and climbed onto a broken white outdoor table and looked into the window. Her father was still reading the newspaper. Isla grinned, jumped off the table, and silently ran toward the barbed-wire fence. One part of the fence was broken, and she could fit through it with ease. She ran to the best climbing tree she had ever found on the property and climbed to the top to watch the sunset. She settled on a wide branch and swung her legs back and forth over the edge. One of the mockingbirds she'd seen earlier perched on a branch a few feet above her and began to play their little game. Isla responded to its songs while she watched the sun. The sky began to turn pink, then purple, then blood orange. She tucked her tangled hair behind her ears as she watched with amazement.

After the show was done, Isla carefully made her way down the tree and back through the fence to her home. She arrived just as her father called her for dinner. He had microwaved some leftover chicken and mixed vegetables. Isla sat at her usual place at the wood table in the kitchen, and her father set down their plates.

He took off his glasses and hung them on his shirt as he sat down. "Isla, tonight I want you to bless the food. Don't worry, the Lord will understand every word you say."

He bowed his head and waited. Isla gulped. She knew God would understand, but she still didn't want to mess up.

"Thank you, Lord, for this food and day. Amen," she quickly tried to say. But her father had obviously not understood, because he continued to bow. After a moment's silence, he looked up and realized she was done. Then they ate. Isla dove into the chicken; her dad did a fake cough and looked at her fork. Isla looked at her dirty hands and quickly corrected herself. She didn't worry about becoming sick, for she had a well-built immune system. But her parents still wanted her to use manners, even if she was a little wild inside. While her parents sometimes had difficulty getting her to use silverware, though, they never had trouble getting her to eat her vegetables: she had learned the value of greens from her deer friends and made sure she ate every last one.

The phone rang, and her dad wiped off his mouth with a napkin and then got up to answer it. Isla put her plate and fork in the dishwasher and put up the leftovers while he talked. He seemed to be solving a work problem.

Isla walked to her room and changed into her dad's old company shirt; it served her well as a nightgown. She crawled into bed. Tomorrow was a school day, and she wouldn't be allowed to sleep outside. Isla had school four times a week at 5:00 a.m. till her dad left to work at 6:30 a.m. She also had a program on the old computer in the living room that would help her practice reading and math. Her dad had her do another program for at least an hour every day to help with her dyslexia and speech impediment. Sometimes it felt she was improving far too slowly, but at least it helped. Before she turned out her nightstand lamp, she brushed, and brushed, and brushed, and brushed her unruly hair. Isla yawned. It was about 8:30 p.m., and she was already tuckered out. She turned off her lamp and curled up into a comfortable position. As soon as her eyes shut, she was asleep.

CHAPTER TWO

Isla crawled out of bed and across the hardwood floor to her clothes. With bleary eyes and crazy hair, she sat down and put them on. She tried to keep from washing her outfit because it masked her human smell. Fresh, clean clothes would scare the animals or give her location away. She opened her door, walked to the coffee table in the living room, and sat on her knees while she waited for her dad. She was so tired, she didn't even notice that she was sitting in the dark. Her dad came in, all groomed up in his nice red Western shirt and jeans for work. He flipped on the light switch, practically blinding the sleepy Isla, and joined her.

He put on his glasses and picked up Isla's grammar book. "OK! Looks like we are learning about direct objects, and it looks like diagramming is going to be a bit harder."

Isla sat down and pressed her head up against the side of the table.

Her dad patted her knee. "This won't be too bad! At least you aren't to conjunctions yet."

"Conjunctions?" Isla exclaimed as her head shot up and her eyes opened wide.

"Never mind, you'll learn about those later," he reassured her.

Her dad tore out her work page for the day. "Now, write your name, and follow along as I read at the top of the page."

Isla did so, in messy handwriting that could use some work. Her dad held his finger where he read to help her know where he was. Isla had had just about enough of this thing called grammar. Just when she thought she was done, it always got harder. But her dad taught her the questions to ask to make it a little easier. "See, on this one you would say, 'Sarah threw what? The ball.' Then you just add the direct object to the diagram, like this," her dad explained.

Isla nodded her head and started to try it.

"Good! You got it! Now let's go over math," her dad said as he checked his watch.

Isla was a bit behind in math and still learning some basic division. She'd understood it until they'd begun long division. Just looking at the problems now overwhelmed her. She couldn't seem to figure out how the answer was found. The only way she could get one right was by following every single step with her dad. Even with him right there directing her, she sometimes messed up, and he'd have to stop her and have her redo the step. For now, that was all they were working on, plus a few reviews here and there.

After math, they did a little science. This was Isla's favorite because her dad let her pick the topic. Of course she chose animals. It was absolutely fascinating to her, learning how their bodies worked and why they did the things that they did. It helped her learn new techniques in running, climbing, socializing, and even hunting. She had even learned to move her arm like a squirrel's tail to communicate with the squirrels on the prairie.

Isla's dad closed the book and stood up. "I gotta go to work. Do the rest of the math and grammar while I'm gone."

He kissed her forehead, grabbed his black workbag and keys, and walked out the door. Isla still wasn't sure what her dad did for a living. She had visited him frequently at work when she was younger, but all he did was sit at a desk, talk on the phone, and type on his computer.

One day when she was four, she had climbed onto his lap, ready to see what fascinating wonders lay on the screen of his big computer. But it wasn't fascinating at all. All she'd seen was him scrolling through a bunch of words in black and white. Disappointed, she had climbed off of his lap to wander around his boring office. In her opinion, it had needed more color, so she'd found yellow highlighters, blue pens, red pens, Expo markers, Scotch tape, and copy paper. She had gathered her findings on a small, round, wooden table and let her imagination take over. She'd made life-size drawings of herself, animals, and plants. Since her dad wouldn't allow her to use his huge scissors, she'd had to carefully tear the pages. Then, she had assembled them all over the wall. People entered the office and gasped while Isla sat crisscross applesauce on the floor, hardly noticing them as she gazed at her creation. She had covered the walls in messily drawn barbed wire, trees, flowers, berry bushes, squirrels, deer, hogs, coyotes, mountain lions, bobcats, armadillos, opossums, snakes, mice, turtles, frogs, lizards, and bugs—and one life-size drawing of herself. At the end of the day, her dad had stood up and just about fallen over when he'd seen the walls. He'd been so busy, he hadn't even realized just how much drawing she'd done. It had been one of her proudest days.

Isla stopped daydreaming and walked to the window. The sun had already begun to rise. She watched her dad drive down the road in his white pickup truck, dirt flying behind him. Ferdinand was still lying down in the shade of her mom's little old blue car, watching the pickup disappear into the distance with his floppy ears perked up. He leaned his nose forward into the sunlight to sniff the air. His white-streaked muzzle had a sort of glow in the early morning light. Isla turned around and got back to work. It took what seemed like forever to finish. She really wanted to go outside and see if the squirrels were out and about. It had been two weeks since she'd last seen them. The three squirrels she loved the most were Sammy, Piper, and Acorn. Sammy was big and bushy, Piper was slim and long, and Acorn was small and had a thin tail. These squirrels were the easiest to interact with.

Isla finished, threw her pencil down on the table, and darted for the door like a caged thing released. Ferdinand jumped when Isla came running out of the house and watched her as she ran down the dirt road to Sammy's tree. It was the closest squirrel tree to her house. All she had to do was crawl through the broken barbed wire and continue northwest for about five minutes. His tree had a big hole near the top and a back door at the bottom. Isla ran to it and made a little chirping noise that she had learned to imitate. Sammy's head appeared in the top opening. His nose rapidly twitched, and his black, beady eyes were full of curiosity. He cautiously made his way out of his safe hole, taking sudden little steps until he looked down at the smiling Isla and ran down the tree to crawl up her shoulder. Isla giggled and watched as he sniffed her for food.

"I've got nothing today," she laughed.

He soon found that she didn't and hopped down to the ground in front of her. He stood up on his hind legs and watched her. Isla moved her arm like a squirrel tail and invited him to forage with her. He moved his tail in response and then led her to some acorn trees. Isla went up one tree and he went up a different tree. Sammy perched himself on a branch and started to stuff his furry cheeks with acorns. Isla got comfortable on a big branch and started to pick acorns, using her shirt as a pouch. Her stomach started to grumble. Once she had enough acorns, she would eat about five small ones. The acorns were very bitter if eaten raw and could be toxic if she ate too many. Isla would eat little handfuls of small ones every once in a while and no more.

Her mom had taught her to cook them a few years ago. When cooked, they tasted sweet. But Isla wasn't going all the way back home just to cook a little handful of acorns. Besides, she had a high tolerance for bad-tasting food. After a while,

Sammy hopped to Isla's tree and started working on another branch. His cheeks were stuffed, and Isla couldn't see how he could hold anymore. After picking a few more, she carefully slid down the tree. Sammy ran down the tree, jumped onto her shoulder, then jumped to the ground and ran back to his tree. Isla followed and laid most of her acorns by his back door. She took one last look at Sammy before leaving to go find Piper's tree.

She started eating acorns as she walked. Each time she stuck one in her mouth, she would make a sour face and force it down. Fortunately, to Isla's delight, before too long she came across a few blackberries. The berries were both tart and sweet. They tasted far better than acorns. Isla stopped to eat a good couple handfuls of the beautiful berries. Now her stomach had just about settled. Once she eventually made her way to Acorn's tree, she would pass a creek with fresh water, and she could not wait to drink from it.

Piper's tree was a bit more concealed than Sammy's and harder to find. It was about a thirty-minute walk from Sammy's tree. It was on the side of a long ditch that had been a creek before the onset of this drought. Isla knew how to find it because it was next to an old, dead tree that had been struck down by lightning about a year ago. Underneath this tree was a rattlesnake's den. Isla had to be careful and watch her step when she passed it. She called the snake Ruckus because he made so much noise. He'd had gone after Isla a few times before, and at first it had been scary, but now she looked at it as an opportunity to practice escaping—but only if Ruckus happened to go after her. She knew far better than to toy with a snake.

Isla walked around the tree, constantly watching the ground underneath it. Suddenly, Ruckus started to rattle.

"Well, 'good morning' to you too," Isla said sarcastically.

She could see Ruckus now. He was curled up, but not in a striking position. He knew not to mess with Isla, just like she knew not to mess with him. She wouldn't call him a friend, but he was a sort of ally. They had a healthy respect for each other. He watched her as she carried on to Piper's tree.

Isla found Piper's home and made the chirping noise. She held her breath and waited. Piper came running down from somewhere in the top of her tree and darted back inside her hole. Then, hanging on to the edge of the hole with her front paws, she leaned forward toward Isla's face. Piper's home was just as high as Isla's face, and she was almost touching her. She went back into her hole. After a few moments, she came out with a baby squirrel in her mouth.

Isla gasped and muttered, "You're a mother now!"

Piper put the kit down and went back and forth, bringing out each kit to show Isla. Isla counted three in all. She began to ponder what she would name them. But the kits were blind and furless, and it was impossible to tell their sexes yet. Piper started to care for the kits, and Isla decided it would be best for her to leave.

Acorn's tree wasn't too far from Piper's. He lived in two trees that had become conjoined over the years. The two had started

separate, but as they grew, they became one. It was amazing, and Isla hadn't believed it when she'd first seen it. Acorn's hole was high up in the fused tree. As Isla made her way to it, she thought more about names for Piper's kits. If she could visit enough, eventually they would be just as tame as their mother. She couldn't help smiling as she imagined holding the young squirrels. They would start to leave the nest in about eight weeks, and Isla couldn't wait.

She found the creek near Acorn's tree and finally satisfied her thirst. It was very thin and only about three inches deep, but it still continued to flow and provided vital fresh water. Isla called it Acorn's Creek and had even carved the name into a fallen branch with a pocketknife and laid the branch by the edge of the water. She had been quite proud of herself for being able to do so. The sign looked like this: "Akornz Kreak." It had looked about right to Isla when she was nine years old, but now she was sure she'd spelled it wrong.

Acorn's tree came into view, and Isla began to make the chirping noise. Acorn peeked out of his hole. He had grown bigger since the last time she'd seen him. But his tail was still recognizably thin. He was a bit skittish. He had learned to trust Isla at a young age but was a bit unsure now. Isla moved her arm to tell him she was a friend. Acorn made small, sudden movements as he went down the tree. Isla crouched down and offered him an acorn. He slowly took the invitation and walked up to her. Acorn had been known to accidentally bite, so she laid the acorn in front of him. He took it up in his tiny paws and broke off the shell to eat it. Once he'd finished, he crawled toward her extended hands and sniffed them.

"That's all I have," Isla informed him.

Acorn jumped onto Isla's knee and looked at her for a moment. Then he scampered off back to his tree. Isla looked at the sun. It was about 11:00 a.m. She started to head back home. The wind blew through the leaves of the trees and relieved Isla's neck of its blanket of hair. Isla made a disgusted face, remembering it was bath night. She felt like baths were a waste of her time and always got shampoo in her eyes. She didn't mind it as much when it got really hot. In the summertime, her hair acted as a wet blanket and kept her cool in the night. If she didn't shower before bed in the summertime, she would find herself tossing and turning all night, sweating because of the heat.

Isla's feet began to ache. She had been walking and standing for hours. She would have loved to take a dip in the pool at the end of her favorite creek, but it was way too far from here, and she needed to get some work done on the computer. A red-tailed hawk flew above Isla's head. It was a female. Isla stopped and debated whether or not she should follow it or go home. She was curious to see if this hawk had a nest of babies. She had seen baby birds of many different species, but never hawk babies. Isla gave in to curiosity and followed. The hawk looked like she was getting ready to land.

Sure enough, she landed nearby on a tree. Her nest was huge. Isla reflected that she could sleep in that thing! The male was there as well, and little noises could be heard from the nest.

Isla climbed a tree a little distance away and tried to see the young hawks. They were fuzzy and had not started to grow little feathers yet. Isla loved the fact that the whole family was together. Some species of animals around here never knew their fathers, so the hawks together were an amazing sight, but she knew she had to get going. Her father expected all of the day's schoolwork to be done, so she quietly left the little family of hawks.

Isla looked at the sun and realized another hour had already managed to go by. She ran through the trees, jumping over sticks and thorny plants. Soon she saw Ruckus's dead tree, but he wasn't there. So she ran right up to it and jumped over it. It felt good to not have to be cautious around that old tree. She was running without a care in the world until something made her stop dead in her tracks.

There was something glistening in the grass ahead of her. Something that had not been there before. She looked all around her and slowly approached it. It was a computer disc, but it had no writing on it. Although it was slightly scratched, it was not only in one piece but also fairly clean. It couldn't have been there for long. Isla picked it up, beginning to feel tense. While she had been having a great time visiting the squirrels, she had not been alone.

"Isla, you're just jumping to conclusions," she told herself. "A bird just probably dropped it or something. You're the only one that's been out here."

Her stomach started to feel like it was tied in a knot at the thought of someone else out on the prairie, possibly watching her. Isla hummed a few songs to calm herself as she walked on. A few mockingbirds joined in, which comforted her. If they were calm, then she should be too. And if they flew away, then she would know she was in trouble after all.

She was only about half an hour from home, but it felt like days away. She had never been afraid of animals, but she definitely feared humans. She didn't spend a lot of time with them, but she knew their free will made them unpredictable in ways animals just weren't. Animals had instincts, and if they wanted to kill you, they had to run to you. A human could kill you from a mile away. Isla had read tales of terrible people in books and in newspapers. She shook her head. All those stories had made her paranoid, she thought. She was just making things worse for herself.

As Sammy's tree came into view, Isla let out a huge breath of relief. She started to run again and soon found the barbed-wire fence. She crawled through it and ran up the dirt road. Ferdinand hobbled toward her as he panted, and he slowly wagged his tail like usual. Isla ran to him and gently hugged him. He sat down and rested his head on her shoulder.

"You have no idea how happy I am to see you," she said, watching his tail swing from side to side.

Isla got up and went inside. For a second, she had feared someone might be in the house. But she knew Ferdinand wouldn't have been so quiet and relaxed if someone had come into their home.

Isla had never thought she would be so happy to sit at the computer to do her homework. She put in her school disc. As she waited for the old beige computer to load her program, she fiddled with the disc she'd found out in the fields. She wondered what would happen if she put it in the computer. But this disc could have anything on it, so she hid it behind the computer. It could be music or a movie, but it could also be some sort of dangerous computer program. Isla did her best to forget about it as she started her schoolwork.

It was probably nothing anyway. At least, that's what she hoped.

CHAPTER THREE

"Isla, could you come here for a minute," her dad called from the kitchen.

Isla put her grammar homework down beside her and hopped off her bed. She was a little uneasy as she walked to the kitchen. She didn't like the tone in her father's voice. It had been three days since Isla had found the disc. She hadn't noticed anything else suspicious going on in the woods, but she wasn't going to relax just yet, and she wondered what was going on. She walked into the kitchen. Her dad was sitting at the table and pulled out a chair for her to sit.

He took off his glasses as she sat down. "My old friend Robert has invited me to his wedding," he said. "When I asked for gift ideas . . ." Her dad paused, as if unsure how to go on. "He said that all he wanted was to finally meet you."

Isla gaped as the room suddenly started to spin and turn black and white. Then everything went black.

Isla opened her eyes. It was bright, and she could barely make out the dark figure leaning over her. Her ears were ringing, and she could hear echoes of what sounded like her name.

Isla blinked, and everything started to fall into place. She gasped. "What happened?"

"You passed out after I told you about the wedding," her father said as he helped her up off the floor and back onto her chair. "Are you dizzy? Do you need some water?"

He felt her head to see if she had a fever.

"I think I'm OK," Isla said as best as she could, a little confused. She'd never fainted before; she'd always thought people only fainted if they were hit on the head.

"I'm going to get you a glass of water. If you feel even a little dizzy, immediately shout for me," her father said as he walked to the sink.

Isla leaned her head back against the chair as she thought about having to go to a wedding. Her stomach started to turn. She really didn't feel comfortable going to a place filled with people. She was barely over four feet tall and only eleven years old and feared that a crowd of adults could practically swallow her. And then there was the talking! Whenever she went out, people always tried to talk to her, and when she couldn't answer, they'd just stare. It made Isla just want to run and hide in a tree or something. She hadn't gone to a public place in two years, and she didn't want to go now.

Her dad handed her a glass of water and watched her drink it. "Feeling better?"

"Yes," she said as she set the glass down. "Do I really have to go?"

Her father gave her a confused look.

She cleared her throat and slowly repeated herself.

Her father looked at her. "Yes. I talked to your mother on the phone, and we think it would be good for you to get out."

Isla groaned and leaned back into her chair again.

"Oh, and your mother wants you to get a dress for it."

Isla's eyes widened, and she shot up in her chair. "A dress?"

Her father laughed. "Calm down! We don't want you fainting again. I'll take you shopping later today and let you have full control over which dress you wear. Even if it's the dullest shade of gray."

"All right," Isla said, mustering up the most pitiful look she could imagine.

When her father did not relent, she stared down at the table. Her dad opened his arms to her, and she stood up and hugged him.

He wrapped his big, safe arms around her and rested his chin on her head. "You'll do fine. I'll do all the talking for you."

Isla loosened her grip so she could see his face.

"Promise?" she asked as she looked up at him.

"Promise."

The mall was *huge*. Isla couldn't believe her eyes as she gazed out the window of her dad's old pickup truck. It was the size of Texas compared to her house. They might as well put streets on the inside. Her dad parked the car among hundreds of cars that Isla had never seen before. She had always thought there were only a few different types of cars. Isla got out on her dad's side. One of her shoes fell off as she jumped out. Without any shoes of her own, she was wearing her mother's boots. They were terribly big on her; she had to focus on walking just to keep them on.

A stampede of cars went back and forth across the road. Isla grabbed her dad's hand. She was sure they'd get hit any second. They started to cross. A car honked, and Isla jumped. She edged even closer to her father as they went on and walked into the mall.

Everyone was so fancy. People actually did their hair and dressed in nice, horribly uncomfortable-looking clothes. Everybody stared at her. Their eyes on her left her blushing in confusion. She probably looked like something the cat dragged in, she thought. One lady looked shocked as she stared at Isla's messy hair. A spoiled-looking little girl looked disgusted when she saw Isla's boots. Her father sighed. Isla could tell he had noticed everyone staring at her. She felt as though she might even cry.

Her dad stopped and looked down at her. Isla hugged him and buried her face into his shirt, desperate for everything to just disappear. Her dad sighed and slowly crouched down until his eyes aligned with hers.

"Those people are probably just jealous that you get to dress like you do. Their parents would never let them leave the house like that," her dad reassured her.

"You think so?" she whispered.

"Yep. They don't know what it's like to not have to check their hair every ten minutes. They don't know what it's like to not have fancy shoes constantly torturing their feet. I'm sure they all want to be you right now."

It was probably a lie, but it helped anyway. "Don't forget, they also have to shower like *every day*!"

Isla's dad laughed, "They sure do!"

Isla felt a lot better now. Her dad stood back up and offered her his hand. She grabbed his hand—but not as tight as before. As they continued to walk, she looked around. There were stairs that magically moved, and the floor was so perfect it actually shined in the light. Isla wanted desperately to just lie on it. They walked out of the clothing store they'd entered through and stepped into a huge room. It had moving stairs everywhere and a huge fountain on the bottom story. Sunrays shined through the glass in the ceiling, and stores were lined up everywhere.

They walked by an entire store just dedicated to selling wristwatches. The next store had very little lighting and was filled with teenagers buying clothes. They turned the corner, and the mall opened up even more. Isla looked to her right. There was a huge dining area with food stands lined up side by side surrounding the tables and chairs in the center of it all. She hadn't known people could buy food in a mall. Isla's dad led her over to some of the moving stairs.

Isla stopped and held her dad back. "Wait, what are we doing?"

"Come on, Isla," her dad said. "The escalators will get us downstairs faster. Here, follow my lead."

He walked onto the first step, and Isla stumbled after him, afraid of getting stuck at the top without him. She'd never been on an escalator before. She clutched her dad tighter as she noticed the stairs disappearing at the bottom.

Isla eyed the bottom of the stairs with suspicion. "Will it suck us in?" she wanted to know.

Her father looked confused. "Will it what?"

"See where the ground sucks the stairs in?" she explained, pointing to the bottom.

Her dad chuckled a little. "It's not sucking them in. They were designed to move into the ground and come back through again. Don't worry, we're too big to go with them."

Isla still watched the ground as they neared. Her dad stepped over the place the stairs vanished into the floor, but Isla jumped over it. She wasn't taking any chances. They walked by a large cart covered with cages full of rodents. Isla looked at the caged animals with confusion and horror. Who would cage an animal and then show off their catch to thousands of people?

Her father noticed she was upset. "That's a pet store, Isla. You know we have Ferdinand. Some people prefer pet rabbits. People breed animals then sell the babies to caring owners."

"Oh," Isla said as she watched them, but it still didn't seem quite right to her. She wondered why anyone would want to see an animal caged rather than free. Running through the woods foraging with a rabbit seemed far more fun than just putting food in a cage. They walked on and passed a cart with tiny airplanes. One was even flying around.

Isla eyed them. "Those aren't real planes, are they?" she said skeptically.

Her father pointed over to the side of the cart. "Remote-controlled. You see that man with the box in his hand? He controls the plane with the buttons on the box. It's a toy."

"Oh," Isla said.

They walked on, and a children's clothing store soon came into view. Isla didn't like the snow-white statues modeling the clothes in the window. They were scary—if she stared at them too long, they appeared to move. They walked in, and some kid's radio station was playing.

The store was very colorful. In the center, there was a big table with blocks that you could actually stick together. She watched a boy put some together until he made a robot-like thing, but eventually, they had to start looking at the clothes. They found the dresses, and Isla immediately shook her head with fear. They were so glittery and itchy looking.

"See anything yet?" her dad asked as he looked around.

"Nope," Isla grumbled as she scrunched up her nose at a big, frilly dress.

"Look over here, these are more simple," her dad called, showing her some dresses that weren't so bold.

Isla looked at them. They were more simple but still not simple enough. Then she saw it. A plain white dress with tiny straps. There was no pattern, and the material was light and soft. There were no fancy designs, no frills, and it even had built-in shorts.

"This is the one," she declared as she felt the fabric between her small fingers. Her dad took a dress off the rack and held it up to her.

"This looks about right. Want to go try it on in that changing room?" He pointed over to the back of the store.

Isla could not believe the words that had just come out of her dad's mouth. She also could not believe the people she saw back there actually *doing* it! Changing clothes, in *public*! "Change clothes, *here*?"

"Yes. You do it to make sure it fits, so you don't have to exchange it."

Isla rapidly shook her head, horrified. "I think it fits just fine!"

She turned and headed toward the cash register.

"All righty then, but if it doesn't fit, we will be back here very soon," her dad warned. Isla just shook her head again.

Her dad paid for the dress and picked up a white bow about the size of Isla's hand that was in a box on the counter. She looked up at him, confused, as he put it next to the dress. Isla pushed her hands against the side of her face as she realized she would have to wear it.

"Oh no," she muttered as the lady bagged their stuff. But as they walked back through the mall, she didn't grab her dad's hand.

After walking a little ways, she asked, "When is the wedding again?"

"What?"

Isla looked down, frustrated. She hated having to repeat herself all the time. "The wedding," she said again. "When is it?"

"We will leave the house at about 6:30 tomorrow evening, but the drive will take a couple of hours. The wedding starts at 8:30 tomorrow night," her dad replied.

They walked on, and Isla bit her lip as she thought about the wedding again. She had hoped to spend the night outside tonight, but that was obviously not going to happen if she had to look nice tomorrow. Isla jumped onto the escalator, and one of her boots fell off. As they went upstairs again, Isla picked it up and put it back on, and her dad looked at her curiously.

"Oh! Isla, I almost forgot shoes!" he exclaimed.

She had never even thought of that. She slouched and looked at the ground.

"Not shoes," she muttered.

Isla thought about having to wear shoes as they walked across the magnificently smooth floors upstairs. They walked into a shoe store. Looking around, Isla was amazed by how many kinds of shoes they had. Around her house, she'd only ever seen flip-flops, sneakers, and Western boots. They walked over to the girls' section, and Isla's mouth opened wide as she saw row after row of different shoes.

"These look nice," her father said as he led her to some dressy sandals, like the kind her mother used to wear to church.

Isla made a face, imagining having to walk in shoes like that. Some were an inch tall. One had four straps that all crossed each other. Others had huge, sparkling flowers on top. Finally, she spotted some plain summer flip-flops in a basket.

"Over here," she said, calling her father over to look.

They both started rummaging through the basket full of different-colored flip-flops.

"These are perfect," her dad said, holding up a white pair that matched her dress.

Isla slipped them onto her feet. It was strange, but they seemed to fit.

Isla sighed a breath of relief. "Now we can go home."

Isla looked at herself in the mirror. She hardly recognized herself. Her brown eyes and freckles were the same, but everything else was so different. Her hair was combed, she was squeaky clean, she was wearing a dress, and she had shoes on.

"If you're ready, I'll come do your hair," her dad called.

Isla's eyes opened wide, remembering that bow. She didn't want to wear that!

"You know what, I think I forgot to do a few things."

Her dad could always tell when she was lying. "Isla, open the door," he said.

Isla took a deep breath. "OK."

When she opened the door, her dad gasped. "You look beautiful!"

Isla waved her hand at him, annoyed.

"Seriously, you look amazing."

Isla huffed. "Thanks," she said grudgingly. She hadn't wanted to wear a dress or get fancied up at all. Her dad walked into the bathroom, picked up her hairbrush, and gently brushed out Isla's damp hair. He then reached in the cabinet for a hair tie.

"How about I attempt one of those cool braids that starts up here and—"

"No, no thank you!" Isla interrupted, waving her arms back and forth.

"All right, I'll just do a ponytail," he said as he got to work.

It felt so unnatural to tie her hair back, Isla thought. "You know, you really don't have to do my hair at all," Isla told him. "Isn't the dress enough?"

She could hear the smile in her dad's voice as he replied. "That's what I said, but your mom wants it done for tonight."

"Sssssssst!" Isla made a sour face as her dad did her hair. It hurt, and she didn't like it.

"Whoops, tangle! I'll be right back," he said, securing her ponytail with the hair tie.

He returned with the bow and put it at the top of the ponytail.

"Ta-da!" her dad said as he stepped back to admire his work.

Isla had to admit it didn't look bad.

"Thanks," she said, a little reluctantly. She was still mad that he was making her go to the wedding at all.

"You are very welcome," her dad replied as he left to go get ready.

Isla turned off the bathroom light and walked into the living room. She sat at the computer and got a little work done while she waited. Her dad didn't want her going outside and getting dirty, so she figured some math practice just might help pass the time. Ferdinand barked, and Isla realized he needed to be fed. She fetched his scoop of kibble and walked outside. The noise of her flip-flops soon became unbearable. Even Ferdinand turned his head to the side and watched them as she walked. Now she saw why they called them flip-flops, because they went 'flip, flop, flip, flop,' everywhere they went. Isla filled Ferdinand's bowl.

"So, I'm going to a wedding tonight. Wanna come?"

Ferdinand looked at her and turned his head to the side.

Isla wrinkled her nose. "I know, I'm actually going some-where! You don't realize how good you got it, staying outside all day and never having to return to civilization."

Ferdinand wagged his tail as he finished his bowl.

"OK, now you're just rubbing it in," Isla said with a smile.

She thought back to the last time her mother had taken her somewhere. The memory still haunted her.

She was nine years old. They were running errands, and the store was crowded, but there was an area made just for kids with a TV playing a movie, toys, colorful beanbags, a bench, and some books. It was surprisingly empty, considering how packed the rest of the store was.

It looked interesting, and way better than the crowded grown-up store, but when Isla's mom told her she could wait there, Isla protested. "I wanna stay with you!" she cried.

"I'll be right back, I promise," her mom reassured her.

Isla watched as her mom walked away. Her stomach started to churn, and she would have run after her mom, but she lost sight of her in the crowd and couldn't tell where she had gone. Isla tried to breathe, tried to calm down. She sat down on the bench and tried to watch the TV, but it was playing so softly she could hardly hear it over the music playing in the store. Why would the store play the music so loud and the TV so softly? She didn't understand the movie, either. It was strange—both live action and animation, with people talking to cartoon animals. She tried to read their lips, but it was too hard.

"Hi, there."

The croaky voice next to her almost made Isla jump out of her skin. She looked up to see a tall man standing beside her. She disliked him at once. He was bone thin, with jet-black hair, baggy clothes, and pasty white skin.

He smiled at her. "What's your name?"

Isla stared at him, heart pounding, but she didn't say a word. She knew better. She wasn't allowed to talk to strangers, and even if she was, she had no desire to talk to him.

"Ah, you're shy. I understand." He sat on the bench next to her. Isla slid away from him.

"It's okay, I'm a nice guy." He paused, as if waiting for her to talk. "You like pets?"

Isla wasn't sure she should answer. Her parents had told her not to talk to strangers, but she didn't want to be rude, either, so eventually she nodded her head.

The man's smile widened. "Good! I've got lots of pets. My favorite pet is my little kitten, Snowball. She looks just like an adorable, fluffy ball of snow. She's out in my car. Would you like to see her?"

Isla didn't budge. She wished her mom would come back already. Her parents had warned her against strangers who offered children things like candy and toys in order to kidnap them.

But the man reached down and grabbed her arm. Isla pulled away and screamed at the top of her lungs. Startled, the man immediately loosened his grip enough for Isla to escape.

"What are you doing?" a deep voice yelled from behind them. An employee had come running at Isla's scream.

"I-I-I didn't do anything, I was just talking to her!" the man stammered.

Isla burst into tears. It was all too much! The two men started yelling back and forth.

"Isla?" her mom shouted, darting out from a nearby aisle.

Isla ran to her as fast as her little legs could carry her. She ran into her mom's arms, sobbing.

"You ready?" her dad called as he walked down the stairs to the truck.

Isla snapped out of her daydream, heart pounding, skin cold and clammy. She calmed as she looked up at her dad. Isla was shocked to see he was in a suit.

He noticed her confused look. "I wouldn't make you dress up if I wasn't going to," he chuckled.

"Oh, well, you look sharp," she said, heading to her side of the truck.

"Thanks, but just like you, I would have preferred my regular clothes," he sighed as he got into the car and straightened his tie.

He made a face as if it were choking him. Isla grinned. It served him right. She buckled up and watched the sun as they drove down the dirt road. She felt like a princess going to a royal ball. It felt both nice and unnatural at the same time. She gazed longingly at her favorite meadow, trying to forget her experience at the store. She knew not everyone was like the man she had met there, and she didn't want that memory to ruin the wedding. The deer watched them as they drove away. She wished she could be with them. They drove up to the gate, and her dad got out of the car to open it. Seizing an opportunity, Isla reached over to honk the horn. Her dad jumped and looked at her sternly. She immediately changed positions and acted as though she had been gazing out the window, but she couldn't hide the mischief in her eyes. Her dad got in and stared at her, smiling with one eyebrow raised.

Isla laughed and came clean. "It was just too tempting!"

Her dad shook his head, more amused than annoyed, and they continued down the road, leaving the gate open. Where they lived, they didn't worry about people trespassing. It also helped that there was a sign on the fence that read "BEWARE OF ATTACK BEAR." Her father had said that it would keep dumb people off their land. For several minutes, there was nothing, just dry, brown fields, but eventually they approached a gas station.

"How do you feel about snacks?" Isla's dad asked, turning on his blinker.

Isla shrugged. "I can eat."

They pulled into the parking lot. Her dad hopped out of the car and headed inside. There was only one other car in the parking lot. Isla assumed it was an employee's car. Isla read some of the signs they had on the window. One read "Water Only Two Dollars Per Bottle!" Isla raised one eyebrow. That was a lot of money. Her dad returned with two bottles of water and some trail mix.

"I got some M&Ms with obstacles!" He said, handing her a bag.

Isla smiled. Her dad had practically read her mind. They headed back down the road, and Isla occasionally popped a bit of trail mix in her mouth. It was all pretty much fine, except for the raisins. She'd liked raisins when she was little, but, thrilled at the opportunity to give her daughter a healthy snack, her mom had spoiled her with so many that she couldn't stand them nowadays.

"Wanna play a game?" her dad asked about half an hour later.

"What sort of game?" Isla wanted to know. She had never heard of a game you could play in a car.

"It's called 'I spy,'" her father explained. "What you do is you see something, like grass, and say, 'I spy something green.' Then I'll try to guess what you see."

Isla looked around. "I spy clouds."

"You can't tell me what it is."

"But they aren't green."

Her dad sighed. "That was just an example. It doesn't *have* to be green. You could say any color, something big, something small, something alive . . . Just use your imagination."

"Oooh," Isla said as she began to look around. "I spy something that lives in dreys."

"Um, what?" her dad asked, confused.

"Come on, think. What lives in something called a drey?" Isla looked expectantly at her father's confused face and giggled. "Give up yet?"

"I got nothing," he admitted, shaking his head.

"A squirrel. I spied a squirrel."

"How was I supposed to know that?"

"Remember, we learned about it earlier in science." Isla said it as if her dad had forgotten her name.

"We learned about squirrels?" her father said, baffled.

Isla made a disgusted noise. "Never mind." She looked out the window. "OK, I spy something that whispers but doesn't speak."

"This is a very advanced version of I spy," her father observed. "Is it wind?"

"Yep," Isla said, pleased he had got it.

"But how did you see wind?" her dad asked.

"Well, I guess what I really saw was the leaves it was blowing."

This was the longest she had ever talked without repeating herself. Her father was finally getting used to her way of talking.

"Now I spy something that can run but can't walk," she continued.

Isla's dad looked around. "Hmm, is it . . ." He looked around some more. "Oh, the creek over there!"

"Yep!"

"Yes!" Her dad pumped his fist in the air and looked quite proud of himself. Isla laughed, and her dad smiled at her. "I didn't know you knew riddles."

"I think a lot," Isla said simply as she rubbed her head. It was starting to hurt from the ponytail.

"Well, I guess you have a lot of free time on your hands," her dad said.

The sun started to go down. Isla looked at the truck's clock. It was 7:54. Isla's stomach started to turn again as she imagined going to a wedding full of people curious to meet her.

"Wanna play another game?" her dad asked when he saw her worried face.

"Sure."

"How about we play a story game?"

"How does that work?" Isla asked before eating a peanut and an M&M.

"I'll say the first sentence of a story, then you'll make up the next one, and we will keep going until we have come up with a story."

"OK, that sounds fun," she said as she ate another M&M.

"Once there was a bear that lived in a forest," her dad began.

"One day, he decided to buy a car."

Her dad laughed, "He bought a car, but it wasn't quite big enough."

"The bear got mad and kicked the car, stumping his toe in the process."

"The bear decided to go to the doctor."

"The doctors tried but couldn't save him, and he died. The end."

"From hitting his toe?" her dad asked.

"It was a really big toe." Isla shrugged, giggling.

Stores and houses slowly began to appear. The sun was just barely on the horizon.

"We aren't too far now. The wedding is in a big church somewhere around here," her dad said as he leaned forward over the driving wheel to look for it.

The games had helped, but the more they drove, the worse Isla felt, knowing they would arrive any second.

"There it is!" her father said as he pulled into the parking lot.

Isla stared at the huge church. The church her mom used to take her to had been a tiny thing. *If this is only a church, what is heaven like?* she wondered.

Although they were early, Isla saw a few cars. She gulped and slouched down into her seat as far as possible. They parked, and Isla felt as though she were at the doctor about to get a shot. In fact, that seemed better right now.

Her dad turned off the truck. "Just so you know, I have told these people all about you and that you wouldn't feel comfortable talking. And I will be there with you the entire time." He looked into Isla's eyes, his soft blue eyes filled with concern and love. Bravely, Isla nodded.

"Well, let's go on in," he said, opening the door.

Isla got out on his side and followed him closely. He shut the truck door and locked it. They strolled down the moonlit path toward the church's big, wooden double doors. A man opened the door for them, and her father thanked him.

Stepping into the church was like stepping into a royal palace. Isla couldn't believe a building like this was located in

Texas. The floors shined, and in the middle was a long, red carpet. They walked down the hallway, and in the center of three paths was a small, beautiful, round marble table. On top was the biggest bouquet of flowers that she had ever seen—as big as she was. Behind the table was a little hallway that led to a bar and dining area. To the right of the flowers was the sanctuary where the couple would be married.

Her father led her toward the dining area, where a few people were talking. A bald, elderly man in a suit glanced over and saw them.

"Christopher! You made it!" he shouted, walking over to say hi.

"How's it going, Darrel?" her dad asked as the two shook hands.

Darrel caught sight of Isla beside her father and gasped dramatically. "This must be Isla!" he cried. Isla blushed. "I haven't seen you since you were a little girl! You used to wander into my office all the time because I had candy on my desk," he laughed.

He reached out his hand, and Isla slowly extended her hand to shake it. Now that she thought of it, he did look a little familiar.

"Your dad talks about you all the time," Darrel told her. He slapped her dad on the back. "You know this guy right here is so lucky to have you as a daughter!"

Isla blushed again and smiled, deciding she liked this guy.

"I sure am," her father agreed, glancing at her, clearly happy she liked his friend.

"My wife probably thinks I got lost again. I'd better go find her. It was a pleasure meeting you, Isla!" Darrel exclaimed before he smiled and left. Isla waved goodbye, and they walked up to another man.

"Isla, this is my best friend, Alexander," her dad said as the man turned around toward them.

Isla looked up at Alexander. He was a very sharp-looking guy, she thought, like the pictures of celebrities in the paper. He had very dark, wavy brown hair that fell just below his ears. He crouched down to her level.

"This is Isla? Nice to meet you. Your dad talks about you so much that I feel as though I've already met you!" he said. His voice was as smooth as butter. He smiled and reached out his hand. But Isla was a little hesitant. Unlike Darrel, she wasn't so sure about Alexander. Something about his eyes made her wary.

After a moment, he dropped his hand. "That's OK," he said. "Soon you and I will be great friends, I can tell."

Isla smiled as he walked off, but she still wasn't so sure about him. He was so handsome and seemed so friendly, but for some reason, she didn't feel like she could trust him so easily.

"I've worked with him since starting my company," her dad told her. "He and I were college roommates before I met your mom. Alexander's like a brother to me."

Isla watched Alexander move away through the people. Maybe she was wrong about him, she thought. The room soon started to fill with people constantly lining up to introduce themselves. Isla felt like a celebrity. Then everyone went into the sanctuary. They sat next to Darrel and his wife, which Isla liked very much. Although Isla had never met any of her grandfathers, Darrel had a loud, friendly way about him that she thought might be what a grandfather was like. She wished he could be her grandpa.

They waited for a while, but it was worth it. When the bride walked down the aisle, it was as if an angel had walked into the room. Darrel nudged Isla and whispered in her ear, "You're next!"

Isla scrunched her nose and shook her head back and forth. Darrel laughed and patted her knee. Both Isla's father's friend and his bride started to tear up as they said their vows. They were pronounced husband and wife, and the two kissed. Everyone stood and clapped, flowers were thrown, and music played. Robert walked down the aisle with his new wife, beaming with happiness.

Isla beamed too. She wanted to have that one day, but she wondered if part of her would ever be happy grown up and married and a wife. Part of her belonged in the forest, she thought. Free. Could any boy ever understand that?

Isla, her father, Darrel, and his wife, Carroll, walked back out to the dining area, and everybody was served grilled chicken, an exotic salad, mixed vegetables, and crème brûlée. Alexander joined them. The adults had a conversation while Isla focused on her food. She had never eaten chicken that tasted so good. Every bite was like a trip to Neverland! The vegetables were amazing too. The salad was all right, but she decided the dressing was a bit strange. But when she first tasted the crème brûlée, it was like heaven in a cup. Isla wished she could eat it every day. The whole world around her seemed to disappear as she ate the magnificent cup of wonderfulness.

Isla was pulled from her ecstasy when her dad nudged her. Isla jumped and looked up at him.

"Isla, Carroll complimented your dress."

Isla smiled at Darrel's wife, very elegant and just as nice as Darrel was. She whispered into her dad's ear. She had to repeat herself a couple times because it was twice as hard for him to understand her when she whispered.

"She says, 'Thank you very much, you look amazing yourself,'" he said to Carroll.

Carroll blushed happily. "Oh, thank you, dear."

Alexander, next to Isla's father, noticed her empty crème brûlée, scraped clean. He smiled and reached for his own dessert. "Here, have mine. My wife wouldn't want me eating it anyway."

Isla gasped and grinned up at him as she took it from his hands. She'd *definitely* been wrong about him, she thought. Alexander was fantastic! She scarfed down more crème brûlée as Robert and his bride walked back into the room. They were in different clothes. Isla assumed they were for dancing. Everyone stood and clapped as the two came in. Isla wanted to see what was happening, but there were too many tall people in the way, so she sat back down and waited for everyone to sit. She yawned and leaned her head against the chair. They all sat down just as the lights dimmed and the music changed to a slow-dancing song.

"Isla, it's already 10:00," her dad said as he looked at his watch. "We'd better go."

Isla nodded and yawned again. She said her goodbyes and even hugged Darrel. But just before they left, her dad took her to meet Robert and his wife. Robert was a short, tan man with dark hair and brown eyes, a bit on the hefty side, but clearly so happy and in love that it made him one of the handsomest men Isla had ever seen. He was delighted to meet Isla and told her that she had made his wedding complete. Isla smiled and yawned once more. She wasn't sure how she had made her dad's friend's wedding complete, but she was too tired to question it. Her dad picked her up, and she almost instantly fell asleep.

Her dad carried her out to the car and buckled her in. It had been a long day, and although Isla tried to stay awake, she was out before they left the parking lot.

CHAPTER FOUR

Isla woke up. She was shocked to find herself in bed. She hadn't woken up to that lovely surprise since she was about five. Isla crawled out of bed and squinted as she walked to the window. It was about 7:00. She couldn't believe she had slept in so late. She got dressed and walked into the kitchen to grab an apple. She munched on its sweet juiciness as she walked outside. Ferdinand got up and followed her for a little bit down the dirt road, but he soon figured she wasn't sharing and went back to the shade of her mom's car. Isla slipped through the barbed wire and laid the core of her apple by an ant bed. Thousands of little workers immediately got to work getting the apple into their home piece by piece.

As she wandered along, she thought about the day before. She had absorbed so much information. The world had grown more technical and complicated. She was thankful that she lived in a calm, peaceful place. Here there were no strangers, no neighbors, and no stores. Just her and the animals. Suddenly, some brush moved in the distance, and Isla realized that she was all alone. There were absolutely no animals around. This meant that a fierce predator was near. Isla had learned that all of the predators were scared of her, so she crept toward the brush to get a better look. She saw a pair of sneakers about the size of her own feet. She reached forward and grabbed the shirt of a boy about her age. His eyes widened, and his mouth fell open, and Isla furrowed her eyebrows and looked him in the eye.

"I'm sorry! I didn't know someone lived here, I was just trying to have fun!" he frantically shouted, surprised by her strength.

Isla looked the boy over. He had blond, wispy hair that fell halfway down his forehead and hazel eyes. He was wearing a Spider-Man shirt, jeans, and shiny red sneakers. "I just moved in not too far from here," he continued to explain frantically. "I got grounded, so I decided to explore and found this cool place."

Isla let him go, and he brushed off his shirt. But despite his evident surprise, he didn't run. Isla frowned. She'd hoped he would run back to where he came from.

"Go!" she ordered him. She didn't say another word. She wasn't about to let him know that she could barely speak.

He ran off, and Isla continued on. But not five minutes later, she heard footsteps behind her. She sighed and turned around. The boy jumped behind a tree, like she hadn't seen him. He eventually peeked his head out and headed toward her. He had a slight, hopeful grin, like just because she hadn't told him to go again she had accepted him as a friend or something. She most certainly had not! She didn't want any other human on the property except her dad and her.

He stopped in front of her. "I'm Cashton, but my friends call me Cash," he said with that hopeful grin. "*We* could be friends!"

Isla shook her head, and he let out a disappointed breath but folded his arms. "OK, but I'm not going anywhere. I have literally nothing to do at my house until I get my iPod back."

"iPod?" Isla accidentally said.

The boy brightened. "Hey, you talk like my little brother."

"You mean you can understand me?" she asked, raising an eyebrow.

"Sure I can! So can we be friends?"

Isla considered it for a minute. "No, I don't talk to strangers." She started to walk off.

He ran after her. "But we've already talked! Just tell me your name, and we won't *be* strangers."

Isla ran and climbed a tree, hoping he wouldn't be able to follow her and would just go home.

"I see what you're doing," he huffed. "I can climb a tree just as good as you!"

He picked a tree and tried to show her. Isla couldn't help but grin as she watched him struggle.

"Just a minute," he said as he grunted.

He'd only made it a few inches off the ground. His hair blew in the wind as he grabbed a branch and tried lifting himself up. He was trying so hard, he was shaking. He fell to the ground, and Isla giggled. She had to admit, it was kinda fun watching him struggle like that.

Encouraged by her laughter, Cashton grinned again, looking up at her in the tree. "You're probably better because you're older than me. I'm only eleven!"

"Me too!"

"Then how about you teach me!" he challenged her, standing and brushing off his clothes.

Isla couldn't help smiling now. She could say one thing for the boy: he didn't give up. "The only teachers around here are the animals," she said, looking around.

She spotted Sammy nearby. She looked down at the boy, imagining his face when she called him over. She made the chirping noise, and Sammy came running. Cash looked confused as he saw what was happening. Isla extended her hand, and Sammy ran up her arm to her shoulder.

Cash's eyes grew huge with amazement.

"You're like Pocahontas or Dr. Dolittle!" he shouted as he watched Sammy perch on Isla's shoulder.

Isla sat as proud as could be with her squirrel friend on her shoulder, enjoying the attention. Ever since she'd learned to call a squirrel, she had always wanted to show someone she could do this. Isla moved her arm to tell Sammy goodbye, and he left for his tree.

"Can you teach me to do that?" Cash wanted to know.

"Like I said," Isla answered as she climbed down and jumped onto the ground. "You learn from the animals."

Cash watched Sammy scampering around by his tree. "But I've seen hundreds of squirrels and haven't learned nothin' from them!"

Isla regarded him for a moment, unable to believe what she was about to say. "Follow me."

Cash skipped a step, happy he'd been accepted. Together they walked through the forest. As they walked, Isla taught him to be quiet and listen, and as he did, she saw his eyes grow big and bright as he began to see the trees, grasses, and animals around them in a different light. It was fun showing him her world, Isla found. It reminded her of when her mother had first shown her, years ago. She showed Cash the creeks, the meadows, even the deer.

"Can you teach me to approach them?" he whispered as they sat on a log on the edge of the meadow under a tree.

"Not yet," she whispered back, staring into his hazel eyes. She'd never seen eyes like his before. Hers were just brown, and her dad's were just blue, but Cash's eyes were all sorts of colors—green, yellow, and light brown all at once.

She looked back at the deer, and she and Cash watched them together as they grazed. She'd assumed it'd be a disaster, taking him to see them, but he'd picked up how to walk in the woods right away, and he'd been just as quiet as she was.

Isla secretly pinched herself. She couldn't believe this. They never got neighbors, let alone someone her age—someone who could understand her! It had to be a dream, but she couldn't seem to wake up, and anyway, how could she have dreamt *him* up, with his iPod and his Spider-Man shirt and his crazy determination? Isla stood and motioned for him to follow. They walked on, and she led him to her favorite tree. She climbed to the first branch and reached her hand out to his to help him up. It was a little weird—she had never let anyone but her parents hold her hand before—but they got on better this way until she was on a good branch and could help him up too. They slid across the branch until their view was clear.

She watched Cash gasp as he saw the sunset putting on the show it put on every night. It looked as if God was painting the sky with every beautiful shade of color known to mankind.

"I've never seen a sunset like this before!" Cash exclaimed.

Isla shrugged. "I guess you haven't ever looked hard enough." She figured he spent most of his time on video games, never knowing what beauty even the simplest things could hold.

Cash nodded in silent agreement, eyes glued to the awesome scene before them. Sometimes beauty was like that, Isla thought. All you wanted to do was look and be quiet. She and Cash swung their legs back and forth, occasionally brushing against each other's jeans. A mockingbird flew into the tree and sang at Isla, inviting her to play their game. Isla joined, aware of Cash's wide eyes upon them.

"Could you teach me that too?" he whispered, quietly like she'd taught him, so as not to scare the little bird singing its heart out on the nearby branch.

"Why don't you try?" Isla whispered back, nudging him in the arm with her elbow.

Cash took a deep breath and thought for a minute. Then he hummed a few notes. They both paused and silently watched to see if the bird would play. It joined in, and Cash let out a sigh of relief with a smile.

He looked back at Isla. "Can I come tomorrow, friend?" he asked quietly.

Isla considered, then nodded. "Isla. My name is Isla," she said.

Cash smiled. "That's a pretty cool name," he told her.

Isla blushed. "Thanks. Yours is pretty cool too."

Isla walked up the moonlit stairs to her house, filled with happy excitement. She had just led Cash back to the gate. Although she hated to admit it, she couldn't wait to see him again. Having a friend was something she had never known before. She'd tried it once, but she wasn't sure she had done it right.

Back when she was five, her mother had taken her to a little church about thirty minutes away. Only a few people went there. Coyote County didn't have a lot of people in it. There were a few other kids there around Isla's age, but she had a hard time interacting with them. The kids didn't like playing with her because they couldn't understand a word she said, but there had been a teenager named Alyssa who had helped with her class and tried her best to play with her.

Isla had loved her; she seemed to be the only one in the church that really cared. But because of Isla's trouble speaking, they'd found that pretending to be animals was really the only thing they could play. Still, Alyssa had been impressed by Isla's ability to perfectly mimic animal calls and behaviors. She'd said it was as if Isla had actually been raised by the animals instead of by her parents. Every Sunday, Isla had scampered after Alyssa on all fours, sitting on her foot and hanging onto her leg as she'd walked around. She'd howled for Alyssa from across the sanctuary, tackled her feet under a table while snarling like a bobcat, and sat on her shoulders while making various bird-calls. She'd caught mice and chased Alyssa while she screamed. Sometimes she'd pretended to be a puppy, guarding Alyssa from boys and screaming like a mountain lion if they got too close, and many other things. To the members of the church, she'd been both annoying and fascinating. It hadn't been uncommon for people to start freaking out when she made predator calls. The other kids and even teenagers had actually grown to fear her. But Alyssa had never been afraid.

After Isla and her mom had been going to the church for about a year, though, the church had had to move because there weren't enough people to support it. From then on, Isla had rarely gone out. At first, she'd missed Alyssa terribly. Isla kicked the ground and wondered where Alyssa was now and what she was doing. She would be an adult now.

Isla walked inside the house. It was dark inside, and Isla started to panic. Her dinner was on the table, and her dad was in bed. She was late! She had never been late and feared being grounded from going outside tomorrow. After a moment, she calmed. It was probably a good sign that her dad was in bed, she thought. He probably would have stayed up to lecture her if she was in trouble. She sat at the table. Her dad had made tomato soup. It was cold, but Isla was too hungry to care. She and Cash had been having so much fun they hadn't even realized they hadn't eaten lunch.

Isla was halfway through her bowl when she remembered the disc.

"What if Cash left it?" she thought.

Just the idea that her friend had left the disc filled Isla with relief. Maybe he would even tell her what it was. She was just dying to know. Isla finished her bowl and put it in the dishwasher. She turned off the kitchen light and made her way to her room. After changing, she looked up at her ceiling and anticipated tomorrow.

"I wonder if that disc is a game? Or maybe music, or even a movie."

Isla went to sleep smiling, imagining hanging out with Cash again and all the adventures they could have together. She still couldn't believe she had a friend.

"I really, *really* don't see the point in this," Cash groaned as he crawled across a dead tree.

"You need to learn to keep your balance!" Isla called.

He was having a bit of trouble. The tree was so uneven that it was hard to keep his balance going across it, especially because part of it was on the ground but most of it was lying against another tree, making it steep.

"Watch me," she said as he got up.

She jumped onto it and ran across the whole thing.

"This will be you real soon if you practice enough," she reassured him.

"But this ain't even climbing, just crawling," Cash complained.

"Baby steps," Isla explained as she jumped down from the top where it crashed into another tree. "What's the point in climbing a tree if you're just going to fall when you get to the top?"

Cash sighed and tried again, but he suddenly shouted and jumped off. "WASP!" he screamed as he ran behind Isla. She couldn't help laughing. He screamed like a girl.

"Don't worry, it's gone now. Try again," she said.

Cash looked all around before trying again. Isla sat in the lush grass, still wet from the morning dew. This was the best place for grass on the property. And the grass that grew here wasn't the weedy grass she was used to; no, this was perfect, lush grass. The trees around the area were the easiest to climb, thin and branchy. She'd figured if Cash was going to learn to climb, he'd better start here. As Cash hugged the tree and slowly slid up the steep part of it, Isla squatted and watched a fuzzy brown spider on a tree stump. It was quite fascinating. The little guy would constantly stop to sort of taste the tree. It would also have to figure out a way to get by every ant it saw. Cash got about five inches off the ground before he stopped.

"Whatcha lookin at?" he asked with a puzzled face as he watched her and held on to the tree.

"A spider," Isla said, never taking her eyes off of it.

"Ew, kill it!" he said with a disgusted face.

"Why on earth would I kill it? It ain't doing no harm!" she demanded, furrowing her eyebrows.

Cash let go of the tree and jumped down. "My momma says to kill any spider you see," he said as he joined her.

Isla sighed. "Watch 'em."

Cash stared at it long and hard. "What about it? It's just walking up the tree."

"But watch *how* he walks. All those bugs got different ways of walking. He looks lost. Maybe he's a hatchling fresh from the egg sack, looking for a place to call home."

Cash watched. "Oh, OK. I see it now."

Isla patted his shoulder. "Good, you're learning!"

Cash looked confused but accepted this was a lesson of *some* sort and didn't say a word. They watched in silence until the spider had become a sort of friend. The spider began to spin a web, and the two smiled.

"Can we visit him tomorrow and see how he's doing?" Cash asked.

"Sure we can," Isla promised.

Cash was learning to have a new respect for nature. If he could learn that, he could learn the animals' ways and eventually do the things that she could.

They walked on through the woods. The ground changed from lush grass to brush. They came across a creek about three feet wide and six inches deep. Isla walked across the cool water to the other side. She turned around to see Cash still on the other side.

"I can't cross in these shoes!" he said with a frown, staring at the flowing water.

"Then take 'em off, for crying out loud!" Isla yelled as she motioned for him to come on over.

Cash hesitated as he took off his shoes and socks. He took one step in.

"Isla, it's slimy!" he whined.

Isla shook her head and walked on.

"Wait! I'm coming!" Cash shouted as he picked up the pace and walked across.

He got to the other side and looked at his wet feet and then his shoes.

"How do I dry my feet off?"

Isla stopped and looked back.

"Just keep walking till they're dry," she replied.

"Till they're what?"

Isla huffed. "Dry," she repeated. "I thought you said you could understand me."

"Well, I can, but I won't always understand every *single* word," Cash said apologetically.

Isla shrugged. "I'm just tired of repeating myself all the time. Come on, let's keep movin."

Cash made weird grunting noises as they walked through the brush. Isla didn't say anything. This was hard for him, she knew, but he always kept going. He watched where she went as he followed. They started to go up a hill. It was so steep that they needed to hang on to the thin trees as they climbed—trees that grew sideways, just like in a book. But as they climbed up, Cash slipped on some leaves, and his foot forcefully slid through a thorny plant.

"AGH!" he shouted, sitting down on the ground and shaking his foot free of the plant.

Isla ran to him, careful not to make the same mistake. She looked at his foot. "You just got a few scratches and thorns," she said. She started taking out the thorns one by one. Cash gritted his teeth every once in a while, but after that first yell, he didn't complain even once.

Isla regarded him, impressed and a little guilty. His feet weren't tough like hers, and she'd told him to walk barefoot. "Your foot is pretty dry now. Go ahead and put those shoes on."

"Thanks," he said as he started carefully putting his socks and shoes on.

As Isla waited, she looked around to see if any animals were in the area. Cash stood, and the two of them continued on. At first, he limped a little, but he hadn't been hurt that bad, and eventually he was beside her once again. At the top of the hill, Cash gasped, and Isla smiled.

The top of this hill overlooked all ten thousand acres her father owned.

The scene was breathtaking. It was as if they were the only humans in the world. Everything was calm and peaceful. They could see deer grazing, birds flying, an armadillo walking into its home, and a lone coyote trotting along a meadow. The rest was too far for the human eye to see. An owl swooped out of the trees above and dove down the hill ahead of them.

"I can't believe I'm seeing this," Cash said as he took it all in.

"I can't believe I get to live here," Isla said. Her father had bought the property a few years before she was born. His company had done very well with his business, and when he'd seen this land for sale, he couldn't help but buy it. They had enough that they could probably live in a mansion like royals, but her father had wanted to live like he'd always had to remind him to be thankful. So he and Isla's mother had fixed up the little white house on the property, and they'd lived there ever since. Isla was always thankful her dad had made that decision when she thought of how she could have grown up. She could have probably become spoiled, spending all her time playing inside the most expensive toys. Instead, she spent her days out here in the magnificence of nature.

"What's that?" Cash suddenly asked.

Isla looked where he pointed. There was something reflecting light a good distance away.

Isla shrugged. "You think it's glass?" The light disappeared.

"I don't know," Cash said thoughtfully. "If it was glass, you'd think we would have seen it this whole time."

"Hmm." Isla looked where it had been. "Whatever it was, it's gone now."

CHAPTER FIVE

"Isla, wake up! You need to get!" her dad frantically exclaimed, pulling back the covers and starting to help her up.

Isla opened her eyes. It was still dark out. She could barely see, but she could hear the quiver in her dad's voice, and it frightened her.

"What's going on?" she asked as she followed him out the door.

"No time to explain! Help me with Ferdinand." Her father held the front door open for her and grabbed his truck keys.

Isla walked out into the dark night, still in her pajamas, wide awake now with fear and confusion. Her dad quickly walked up to Ferdinand. Poor Ferdinand was enjoying a good sleep and had to be woken up. Her dad picked up the front of his body while Isla helped with his back legs. They settled him into the back of the car and quickly hopped in. Her dad immediately started the truck and drove down the dirt road at about forty-five miles per hour.

As they neared the end, Isla opened her eyes wide. Her mouth dropped open. Toward the back of the property, there were fire trucks everywhere. Thick smoke could be seen in the air.

"I got a call from the police just now saying someone had spotted a fire on our land," Christopher said grimly. "But they think they might be able to control it soon."

Isla watched in horror as about an acre of land burned down to ashes. A tear ran down her face. Sammy lived close to these parts. They drove out of the gate and down the road. As they neared Sammy's tree, Isla suddenly couldn't take it anymore. She opened the car door and ran out.

"Isla! Stop!" her dad shouted. He braked hard, threw his door open, and ran after her.

Isla was sobbing as she ran. What had happened to Sammy? Was he okay? What if he wasn't? She put her hands around her mouth and called for her best squirrel friend as loud as she could through her tears. Her dad stopped dead in his tracks, realizing what had upset her, and watched.

"Sammy, please!" Isla muttered as she stared into the fire through her blurry, tear-filled eyes.

Her dad walked over to her and laid his hand on her shoulder. Isla chirped and chirped until she couldn't anymore. She hugged her dad and buried her face into his nightshirt. She could hear the fire, a tree falling, and the shouts of firemen trying to save the land.

"If only we weren't having such a drought," her dad muttered.

Then Isla heard shuffling in the leaves. Her head shot up, and she moved her hair out of her face. Sammy was running toward them a few feet away from the fire. Isla gasped and ran to him. Sammy scurried up to her shoulder. He was breathing hard and smelled of smoke. She gently stroked his fur. She would have hugged him if he weren't so small and if it wouldn't scare him worse than he was scared already. Her sad tears turned to tears of joy and relief. She was so thankful that he was OK. Her dad started to praise God as he watched them. He knew just how much Sammy meant to Isla. He knew not to step forward, though: Sammy didn't trust him.

Half an hour later, the fire was finally out. The ground was black and steaming. A fireman talked to her dad as she watched with Sammy and drank from a bottle of water she had been given. She could see one fireman trying to take a picture of Sammy perched on her shoulder. The firemen had said that it was a sight they'd never seen before. She moved her arm to tell Sammy bye, and he ran back into the forest. Although not a whole lot of land had burned down, it still saddened her, even though she knew that fires could be good for land—they cleared out the dead things and fertilized the ground for new things.

Her dad walked over to the truck and motioned for her to come. Isla ran to the truck and hopped in. Ferdinand was nervously panting in the back.

"The fireman said it appears to have been an accident. Maybe someone threw a cigarette out the car window."

Isla couldn't believe that someone could even think about doing that. It didn't sound smart at all to her, but she knew people like that lived in this world. She sighed and rubbed her eyes as they drove home. The sun started to peek over the hills as they neared the house.

Her dad parked the truck and opened the back door. Ferdinand slowly jumped out and hobbled to his sleeping spot by Isla's mom's car. Isla walked inside. A moment ago, she had feared she'd never see this house again. But it was unharmed, and the only thing new was the smell of smoke on Isla's shirt. She changed into her day clothes and grabbed her mom's old camera from under the bed. It was one of those Polaroid cameras that printed the picture after you took it. She hung the strap around her neck and grabbed some blank photo paper for it. The sun was past the hills by the time she walked outside.

Walking up the dirt road, she imagined how the fire could have started and what would have happened if no one had noticed it. A chill ran down her spine as she thought about the fire swallowing the entire property, including her family. She wondered if it was Cash who had noticed. Not many people lived around these parts. She neared the gate and crawled over it. The air still smelt of smoke as she walked down the road to the burnt area. She took a picture and watched it print out.

"Isla!" a voice called from behind her.

She turned her head to see Cash running toward her. She smiled and watched him run to her. He was wearing old tennis shoes today instead of those nice ones.

He stopped up short as he took in the scene. "What happened?" he asked breathlessly.

"A fire started last night. I thought you called it in," she said as Cash looked at the black ground.

"Nope, not me or my family."

"Hmm," Isla said as she fiddled with her camera. "Want me to take a picture of you?"

Cash looked at her camera. "Whoa, that thing's ancient! Does it really work?"

"Yep! See?"

She held it up to her eye and took a picture of him. Cash did a goofy smile just in time. The picture printed out, and he picked it up.

"It's not as good as my iPod, but it's still pretty cool," he said before handing it to her.

"So what is an iPod?" Isla asked while she put the picture in the camera's bag.

Cash blinked, but when he answered, he didn't comment about her not knowing—something Isla appreciated. "It's like a tiny computer that you can play games on, listen to music, take pictures, text, get on the Internet, and cool stuff like that," he explained.

"Oh, like a smartphone?" Isla asked.

"No, it doesn't make calls, and I have to have Wi-Fi," Cash said regretfully. "I want a smartphone, but Mom says I can't have one until I'm older."

Isla sniffed. "I don't see why you gotta have all that fancy stuff anyway," she said.

Cash looked at her in disbelief. "Cause it's fun!" he cried. "Maybe I'll bring it tomorrow. You'll see!" Isla led him into the brush. "What are we going to do today?"

"You'll see," was all she said.

Cash sighed, but he knew not to question her anymore. So he remained quiet and followed. Isla stopped and looked up at the sky. Cash walked up beside her and looked too. There were dark clouds in the distance.

"Looks like some rain might cool us down today," Isla said. "Good. My dad thinks the fire might not've started without the drought and all."

"My mom doesn't let me go outside in the rain," Cash said nervously.

Isla stopped and looked back at him, confused. "What's she got against rain?"

Cash shrugged. "She says I'll get a cold."

"Pfft, you'll live. We'll be fine as long as there isn't a bunch of lightning," Isla said as she continued.

As they walked through the brush, thunder could be heard in the distance. Isla could tell by the way Cash walked that he was getting more and more nervous. But he didn't complain or turn around to go home. They got onto an old dirt path that had once been a little creek. Every once in a while, they would have to jump down because it had sudden drops.

Then it started to rain, hard. They were quickly soaked. The fresh rain gave Isla chills of excitement. She loved walking in the rain. It was something she rarely got to do. She soon heard strange squeaking noises. She stopped, and Cash walked up beside her as she watched his shoes.

"What?" he asked, looking down at his shoes.

"Why are they doing that?"

"Doing what?"

"Making them noises!"

"Cause they're wet," Cash said, taking one of the shoes off and shaking some water out of the inside.

Isla sighed. His old shoes were better for walking around than the fancy new ones he used to wear, but she still wished he didn't have to wear them at all. Still—she remembered what had happened the last time she'd encouraged him to take them off. His feet were still far more sensitive than hers. It had taken her a long time to get her feet as tough as they were. So she walked on and tried to ignore the sound.

They soon came to a hill. Isla led Cash to the side and into a small cave.

"Wow!" he exclaimed as they walked inside.

The ceiling was only about three feet tall, so they had to crawl. There were old bones everywhere. Isla sat with her legs crossed, and Cash sat next to her. The rain came down like a gentle waterfall over the entrance. It was magical. Isla had never been up here in the rain before, and she knew Cash had never done such a thing.

"What lived here?" Cash asked.

"A mountain lion did a few years ago, but he's gone now." Isla fiddled with a bunny skull. "Wanna know something?"

Cash looked at the bunny skull. "What?"

"One time, my dad told me I could sleep outside in a tent. But after he went to bed, I snuck off and slept in here. He still doesn't know. I'd like to do it again."

Cash looked at her in disbelief. "You slept *here*?"

Isla looked into his hazel eyes. "Yep!"

Cash gave her a "you're crazy" sort of look, which made Isla smile.

"At some point in the night, a few coyotes howled, and I joined them. It was really cool. We should do it sometime."

Cash nodded. "That would be so cool!"

"Have you ever heard a coyote?" Isla asked as she put the bunny skull down.

"Not yet," Cash said, grinning.

"I've been practicing, wanna hear?" she asked excitedly.

"Sure."

Isla howled, barked, and howled again.

Cash turned his head slightly to the side. "That was cool, but do they really sound like *that*? I thought they only howled."

"They howl and make these barking noises, especially when they are attacking something."

Suddenly, a big clap of thunder burst from the sky. Isla and Cash both gasped and watched the lightning. It was much darker now. The rain was pouring down. A cold breeze flew through the cave and gave the two chills.

"Y-you think we should go back?" Cash asked, crossing his arms and rubbing them together for warmth.

"We'll be safe in here," Isla said. She crawled forward toward the entrance.

"Where are you going?"

"I'm thirsty!" she explained.

She put her hands out into the rain and slurped the water out of them. "Um, are your hands clean?" Cash said, with a worried look.

Isla shrugged and continued. From the corner of her eye, she saw Cash lick his dry lips. He was thirsty, too, but he wasn't sure he wanted to join her. Eventually, he shrugged and walked on over. He thoroughly washed his hands off in the rain and then dried them on the inside of his shirt, where it was clean.

"I am not about to get sick!" Cash announced.

They both laughed as he began to get water. Once finished, the two sat back down and lay back against the cave wall. The rain was so calming, Isla wanted to fall asleep, but she didn't want to miss a single moment of this.

"I had to hide from my little brother today so that he wouldn't follow me," Cash said.

Isla looked at him. "Why?"

"I didn't want him coming," Cash said, making a face. "He's only four and so annoying!"

"How?"

"He gets into my stuff, he follows me everywhere, he gets me in trouble, and sometimes my parents let him get away with hitting me. But I can't hit him back!" Cash mumbled something that Isla couldn't quite hear.

Isla was confused. "I thought siblings were a nice thing to have."

Cash looked at her. "Most of the time, it's a nightmare, but sometimes it's all right," he admitted at last.

"So what's your brother's name?"

"Ryder."

"Cool. What does he look like?"

Cash thought for a second. "He's got short, dirty-blond hair, hazel eyes, and wears glasses."

Isla pictured him in her mind. He sounded like a cute little boy. The two continued to talk on and on for hours, laughing and sharing interests. They soon realized it had stopped raining and headed out of the cave.

Cash's stomach growled. "I'm about ready for lunch, but my mom is going to freak when she sees me all wet."

Isla thought as they trudged on. "Maybe you could eat some of our food."

"Well, I don't want to intrude . . ."

"It's fine! You're my friend, and I'm going to help you out," Isla said as they walked into a clearing.

"Thank—"

"Shh!" Isla suddenly interrupted as she stopped and looked around.

A few yards away, a group of hogs was eating.

"Get too close, and those things'll tear you up," she whispered. Cash's eyes widened.

She motioned for him to follow, and they snuck past them.

"How do you know they can?" Cash asked once they were far enough.

Isla stopped and lifted her jeans off her right leg to reveal a long scar that went from the top of her foot up to her knee. "Got up a tree 'fore they could do anything else."

Cash looked at her leg, horrified and fascinated, and then back at her face. She grinned and nodded as he looked at her with disbelief. Then they carried on. Every once in a while, Cash would whip his head back and look around.

Isla eventually turned around. "Trust me, you'll know if they're coming."

He relaxed a bit after that

"So did you go to the hospital?" he asked a few minutes later.

"Well, after they left me alone, I managed to get to the road. My dad found me when he got home and rushed me to the hospital. But the cut wasn't deep enough to do any real damage. I just got a few stitches and medicine for infection. The worst part was staying inside until it healed."

Cash was still impressed. "Wow. I've only gone to the hospital for a broken toe."

Isla turned her head back and gave him a confused look. "You broke a *toe*?"

"My dad accidentally dropped a big hammer on it while he was fixing the fence."

Isla made a disgusted face. "Well, that sounds painful!"

Cash winced and nodded. Suddenly, a huge branch fell right behind him. "Aaaaah!" he shouted as he stumbled forward and ran.

Isla reached out and grabbed his arm. He calmed down, and they looked back at the branch. It was a very big branch. If it had hit Cash, it could have killed him! They exchanged a glance and together breathed a sigh of relief. Then, Isla noticed something strange.

"Cash, look at this!" She pointed at a green X painted on the branch.

"That's what my dad does to dead trees. Maybe your dad did that," Cash said, catching his breath at last.

"He's never done that before, and this tree isn't dead," Isla said, gesturing at the tree the branch had fallen from.

Aside from the fallen branch, the rest of the tree was quite healthy. There were no large, leafless patches; no powdery mildew on its leaves; no missing bark; not even yellow leaves.

"Wait here," Isla said.

"Wait, what?" Cash exclaimed, looking around frantically for hogs.

Isla climbed up the nearest tree.

"Cash, they're everywhere!" she shouted in panic. All of the trees in the area had little green Xes in places where they could hardly be seen. "I *know* we didn't do this!"

Cash looked around, eyes wide, lips trembling. "Isla, you're scaring me; can't we just get home?"

Isla hopped down. They ran the rest of the way. What was going on? Who had been on the property, painting all of the trees? Suddenly, Isla remembered the disc she had found. She stopped up short, seizing Cash's arm.

"Did you ever leave a disc on the property?" she said, looking into his eyes, afraid of his answer.

"Disc? What are you talking about?"

Isla bit her lip. She knew it. She started to run again for the fence. Suddenly she couldn't be home fast enough either. They soon came to the barbed wire and crawled through. They ran up the road, and Ferdinand started to bark, alarmed by their panic.

"It's just me and a friend, Ferdy!" Isla shouted.

Ferdinand stopped, but he stared at Cash suspiciously. Cash and Isla stopped at the door, wiped their feet off, and headed inside. Cash fell onto the old carpet and sat against the wall to catch his breath. Isla sat at the computer to catch hers.

After she'd recovered, she grabbed the disc from its hiding place and showed him. "I found this on the property. If you didn't leave it—what with the marks on the trees and all— someone else's been out there."

Cash swallowed but climbed to his feet and took the disc from her hand. "Does it work?" he asked.

Isla shrugged. Cash's face hardened with resolve. "Well then, let's try it."

CHAPTER SIX

"Wait, wait, wait!" Isla shouted as Cash put the disc in the computer.

He held his finger by the button and looked at her.

"How about now?" he asked, watching her concerned face.

Isla squinted. So many possibilities were running through her head. What if it was a virus, or something that belonged to the FBI, or a video of a murder, or even a bomb! She sat there thinking for a few minutes while Cash waited impatiently.

"OK, just do it!" she said as she closed her eyes.

He pushed the button and stood by her. They watched as the computer started to load. Suddenly, a page popped up. Isla screamed and grabbed Cash's arm. She stopped screaming immediately. She glanced over at Cash. She couldn't believe she'd grabbed his arm! Why had she done that? But Cash had leaned forward, intent upon the screen.

"What is this?" he said.

Isla released Cash, snapping back to reality. She leaned closer. The screen showed a picture of a bunch of pools and slides. Cash scrolled, and cabins came into view. There was a lake and a fishing store, a kayak shop, a refreshment stand, an arcade, some bike trails, and plenty of parking.

"It looks like plans," Isla said as she watched him scroll.

"You think it's plans for a park?" Cash asked. He studied the area with various pools and slides, and he gasped. "Yeah. Hey, it looks like a water park! Look at all of these huge slides, the lazy river, even a wave pool!" He pointed each feature out to Isla as he spoke.

"How can you tell they're huge?" Isla asked, squinting at the screen.

He showed her. "I'm comparing them to that building." He paused and looked at her with growing excitement. "The building that's selling pizza, hot dogs, and hamburgers!"

Isla sighed. "I still don't understand. Why was this on the property? The nearest water park is two hours away. I thought a bird dropped it on the property, but that's a long way to fly."

"Maybe it came from somewhere else," Cash suggested as he scrolled. "Where do you think this place is? I wanna go!"

A few rides and a couple of roller coasters came into view.

"This place has roller coasters!" Cash exclaimed.

"Is there anything else on the disc? Like a name or something?" Isla asked.

They both studied the map. The place was huge. Every time they looked, they saw more activities and buildings scattered across the map.

"Look at that!" Isla exclaimed as she pointed at the screen.

There was a ginormous pirate ship right in the center, towering over everything. It was torn down the middle; the front and back stuck up in the air. It was black on the outside, the inside was dark brown, the sails were white, and it had a red pirate flag. Surrounding the ship was a sort of moat with mermaids.

"Whoa!" Cash exclaimed. "We have *got* to go there!"

"I don't know if this place exists yet," Isla pointed out. "Even if it did, I'm not so sure I'd want to go."

"What? Why? This place looks awesome!"

Isla wrinkled her nose. "But it would be full of people. I don't like going to crowded places, or any place with people at all, to be honest."

Cash thought for a moment. "Would you be OK if we went together?"

"I don't know, maybe," Isla admitted. "But we still don't even know what this place is called or where it might be."

Cash scrolled to the very bottom of the map. In golden letters, it read "Name Pending."

"Pfft, figures," Cash muttered.

"This place doesn't even have a name yet? When do you think this disc was made?" Isla asked.

"I can't find a date, but it couldn't have been made too long ago. Unless, of course, this is an old copy."

"Are there any other words?" Isla asked.

They both studied the screen for a minute.

"What about that?" Cash asked, pointing to the side of the map.

There was a copyright symbol next to tiny letters written in gold that read "Forever Innovation."

"I guess a company called Forever Innovation is making this," Cash said.

Then Isla heard a car pull up. She jumped up and accidentally pushed a few buttons. The computer crashed.

"What'd you do that for?" Cash asked as he looked at her, confused.

"Cash, hide!" she exclaimed as she pushed him toward her room. "My dad is home and doesn't know you exist!"

"What? Why?" he asked as he ran into her room.

"I'm afraid he won't let you explore because it's dangerous," she quickly explained.

Isla casually walked to their brown couch and sat down. Her dad walked in with some papers in his hands and jumped when he saw her.

"What are you doing home so early?" he said as he headed to the kitchen.

"Oh, I just wanted to catch a bite real quick."

"OK, then," her dad said as he gave her a suspicious look.

Isla took a deep breath and tried to look natural. Her dad shook his head and set the papers on the kitchen table. Isla got up and walked to her room. Cash was behind the door. She motioned for him to follow her. He nodded and got out from behind the door. They walked down the old wood-floored hall to the back door. Isla slowly opened it and let Cash out first. As soon as they were out and the door was shut, they took off running down the road. It was a bit muddy, but they didn't stop, even when the mud got in between their toes, squishy, cold, and uncomfortable. In fact, when a hawk came out of nowhere and flew above them, Isla picked up the pace and began to race it. Poor Cash got left behind a little.

But running so fast she left the mud far behind, Isla smiled with joy as she raced the hawk. She felt so wild and free. Her pace only got faster as she tore down the road after the hawk. She was now right under him, and the gate came into view. She readied herself as she neared it. She slid to a stop to keep from hitting the gate, looked up, and smiled. She'd won.

"Isla . . . wait . . . for . . . me," Cash wheezed.

Isla was leaning on the gate, watching the hawk soar. She waited for Cash. He came slowly walking up the road, red-faced and sweating. "Let's not do that again, please."

Isla looked back at him and grinned mischievously. He was breathing like a panting dog.

"You just gotta git used to it!"

Cash gaped at her, and slowly, he shook his head back and forth. "That must have been, like, a whole mile," he said as he walked up to the gate and looked back at the road.

Isla shrugged, "Didn't feel like a mile to me."

"Well you get out more than I do," Cash said as he bent over and put his hands on his knees. "I'm more of a video game and TV person."

"We don't have any of that stuff, just a radio."

"How do you live!" Cash wondered.

"Happily," Isla replied simply, looking out to the woods with a smile.

Cash looked into the woods and nodded thoughtfully. His stomach growled.

"Ya know, we never did eat," he said.

"I guess you'll have to sneak into your house and change clothes."

"Great . . ." Cash said as he looked back at his house with a disgusted look on his face. "But then comes laundry day."

He looked down at his muddy pants and sighed.

"You're a smart boy, you'll figure *something* out."

Suddenly they heard Isla's dad call her name.

"I guess I'd better go," she said.

"OK, bye," Cash said sadly as he slowly started to walk home. "I'll look up that company when I get home!"

"Wait!" Isla yelled. She rushed at him and hugged him hard. Cash jumped and gave her a weird look. Isla blushed and shrugged. "What? We are friends now."

Cash smiled. "Best friends."

Isla ran home with a huge smile on her face. She had never had a best friend before, and it was a great feeling. Clouds started rolling in as she neared the house. It began to rain. She stopped running, stretched her arms out, and spun. The rain soon soaked her hair, and the world seemed to go in slow motion as she looked up into it.

She shouted, "This is the best day ever!"

She looked at her house. Her dad was smiling at her from the window while he held his brown tea mug. Isla blushed and ran to the house. She ran inside and wiped her feet on the rug.

"So," her dad said before taking a sip of hot tea.

"So what?" Isla answered, still trying to act casual.

"What happened today?"

"I played in the rain," Isla said simply.

Her dad sipped his tea again. "Mom sent another letter," he told her.

Isla's eyes opened wide, and she ran to the kitchen. She snatched up the letter on the table and opened it. It read:

Dear Christopher and Isla,

I miss you both so much! It feels like I've been here for years. Grandma Ainsley has been in and out of the hospital for the past couple weeks. She seems to be doing better now, but y'all might want to fly out soon and visit.

There's a little girl who moved in next door with her aunt and uncle. She looks so much like you, Isla! But she's quite the chatterbox. You don't even have to talk to her, she does all the talking for you. I think you two would get along just great!

Do y'all remember those flowers that Grandma Ainsley has been keeping alive for years? They died recently, and she has been complaining unbearably. So I just nod and pretend to listen. But recently she figured I wasn't listening and faked a heart attack. I haven't seen her laugh that hard in years. Apparently I freaked out.

I'm hoping we can come out sometime this summer, even if I have to duct-tape Grandma Ainsley to a wheelchair to get her to come. Goodness gracious, that woman is stubborn!

I love y'all! See you soon!

Love,

Mom

Isla smiled. Her grandmother was pretty hardheaded these days. She giggled as she imagined her mom duct-taping Grandma Ainsley to a wheelchair.

"What does it say?" her dad asked as he walked up beside her.

Isla handed it to him then walked to her room. She took the picture of Cash and put it underneath a photo on the wall. She didn't want her dad seeing it just yet, but she wanted it on her timeline paper. She knew it was weird keeping him a secret for now, but it was nice too. Anyway, she'd never had a friend on the property and wasn't sure how her dad would react. He could make them stop exploring because Cash wasn't used to it like she was and it was dangerous, and on their property, they were responsible for him. But Isla was loving showing Cash the woods so much she couldn't give it up just yet.

After gazing at the picture for a minute, she walked over to her curtainless window and watched the rain. She sat on her knees and smiled as she laid her arms on the windowsill, thinking about her day and about the disc. For the first time in a long time—since her mom had left, maybe, or even longer—things seemed to be going right again. But she wanted to know more about what was going on too.

CHAPTER SEVEN

"What on earth is that?" Cash whispered.

The two were hunkered down in the brush watching a large, white-streaked, brown bird in the distance.

"Roadrunner," Isla replied.

It was about midday. Isla was teaching Cash how to hide from animals.

"It looks like a weird chicken-bird hybrid," Cash said as he squinted at it.

Isla rolled her eyes. "A chicken is a bird, silly. And shhh. You're not suppos' to talk."

The roadrunner perked his head up and looked toward them. He strained his neck to the side and froze. For a couple of long minutes, he just stared at them, trying to see if there was danger.

"It's staring at us," Cash mumbled, trying not to move his lips too much.

The roadrunner took off into the brush, never to be seen again.

"Holy cow, that was fast!" Cash exclaimed as he jumped up to try to see it.

Isla sighed. "We need to work on your quietness."

She stood up, and Cash stood up with her. "That didn't look a thing like that old cartoon," he said as he trudged behind Isla.

"What cartoon?"

"I forgot what it was called, but there was a coyote always chasing this roadrunner."

Isla paused and looked back. "That don't make any sense; a coyote's main source of food is deer."

Cash shrugged. "I guess cartoons don't have to make sense."

Isla nodded thoughtfully and continued. The rain had made the brush grow so high, it was almost up to her shoulders. All she could think about was ticks. The little bloodsuckers were probably all over the place. Poor Ferdinand had already had three. It was also about time for snakes to come out. She had already seen Ruckus, so she knew at least a few were already out and about. Isla looked up and saw a game trail not too far away. She walked toward it. She was getting tired of watching every step she took.

"What kind of animal uses this?" Cash asked as he stepped onto the trail.

"Judging by the size, I'd say coyotes or deer mainly use it," Isla replied. She looked all around for prints and traces of animals. "See this?" She pointed.

Cash walked up beside her and looked at the ground. There were a few faded paw prints in the dirt. "Coyote?" he asked.

"Yep."

"Will they attack us?" Cash asked worriedly.

"If you don't bother them, they probably won't bother you," Isla answered as she walked on. Something white and rusty came into view. "What do you think that is?" Isla asked.

"Looks like a fridge or something," Cash exclaimed.

He ran past Isla to check it out. She watched as he sped off. "Yep, it's a fridge," he called.

Isla jogged up to him. The refrigerator was lying on its back, and the door was missing. There was plenty of murky rainwater inside of it.

"Is it yours?" Cash asked as he walked around it.

"No," Isla said. She looked it over. There was a broken branch underneath it. "I wouldn't get too close. A snake could be under there," Isla warned Cash.

Cash jumped back and looked under it cautiously. "There's no snake, but I see something else," he told her.

He got on the ground and tried to see what it was. Isla handed him a stick. Using the stick, he rolled the thing out from under the fridge. Suddenly, flies flew all around, and he jumped up.

"That's so gross!" he yelled.

Isla walked over to see what all the fuss was. A decaying armadillo was on the ground. The smell started to drift into the air.

Isla wrinkled her nose. "It smells somethin' fierce, too!"

"I almost used my hand to get it out," Cash said, disgusted. His face looked a little green.

Isla put her hand on his shoulder and turned him around. "Let's go before you throw up," she advised.

"Did you see the way half his face looked?"

"Try not to think about it. I don't want you throwing up on me." Isla stepped away from him. She was used to seeing things like that, so it didn't bother her too much.

"When are we gonna head back? It's about afternoon," Cash asked, looking up at the sun.

"In about an hour. I want to show you something first."

"What sort of something?"

"You'll see."

Cash let out an exasperated sigh. Isla grinned. He hated waiting. The property was so big and full of things he'd never seen before.

"Have you ever lived in the city?" Cash asked.

"Maybe when I was a baby, but I don't remember it. What's it like?"

Cash thought for a moment. "It's crowded compared to this place; there's lots of houses and neighbors. There's also plenty of sidewalks to ride a bike on. Sometimes I'd even ride to this nearby shopping center to spend my allowance on a soda and candy bar."

"That sounds cool. It's nearly impossible to ride a bike out here, and there isn't a store for miles."

"I think I'd rather live out here," Cash decided. "There's no annoying neighbors, no traffic, no psychos, and you can do whatever you want outside and no one will see you." Cash raised an eyebrow and flipped over to stand on his hands for a moment to demonstrate, then lost his balance and fell over into the brush.

Isla giggled. "Yeah, I like being able to talk and yell without people judging me," she agreed.

Cash climbed to his feet, brushed off his jeans, and smiled at Isla. "You know, you're getting better at talking," he pointed out.

Isla was pleased. She hadn't noticed. "You think?"

Cash nodded. "Maybe it's one of those things, you know? The more you do it, the better you get. Like walking in the woods. Hey, I almost forgot to tell you something! Remember how I was going to look up Forever Innovation on my iPod?"

"Yes?" Isla gasped, eager to know the answer.

"Nothing, absolutely nothing!" Cash exclaimed.

"Whadd'ya mean?" Isla asked.

"I couldn't find a single thing on it. They haven't made nothin'!" Cash said, clearly disappointed.

"Wow, it must be brand new."

This perked him up. "Hey, I bet that disc was top secret. We're probably the very first people to hear about it."

Isla frowned. "You don't think we'll get in trouble, do you?"

"Why would we?"

"Because no one's suppos' to know about it," Isla explained.

Cash shrugged. "I highly doubt they even know we have it. If we don't tell anyone, how could they ever know?"

"Good point. We'll just keep it a secret," Isla decided.

They continued walking, both silent as they thought about their new secret. It made them feel so important, being the only ones who knew about this new company and their plans.

"We're almost there," Isla said as she looked around.

They were now in an area covered with small trees. They were so low, they had to crawl under them. Isla's hair kept getting caught in the branches.

"What kind of trees are these?" Cash asked after getting scraped by a branch.

"Not sure. Some of them have spikes," Isla replied.

They came upon a small clearing that was covered in brown grass and cacti. Some of the cacti were as tall as they were.

"It's right over here!" Isla cried.

There was a deep ditch that ran like a creek through a few trees. Some of the trees had over half of their roots showing inside of it. Cash stared.

He exclaimed, "I didn't know tree roots were *that* big!"

They jumped down into the ditch and crawled over the waves of roots surrounding them. The walls of the ditch towered over them. Little streams of light shined through the trees all around them. It was as if they'd entered a new world.

"What happened to the creek?" Cash asked

"I never saw it, but it occasionally fills with rain water when there's enough of it."

"Why is it so dry if it rained a few days ago?"

"We're so far into the property, it might not have even rained here," Isla replied while balancing on a huge root. "It is ten thousand acres, remember?"

"I can't believe your dad lets you explore on your own like this."

"He's a little new to this parenting thing, and my mom didn't really worry about me getting hurt," Isla replied.

Isla thought about her mother. She missed her a lot. Her dad hadn't really been around much until her mom had left for Scotland. He'd been too busy working. Her mom had raised her as a stay-at-home mom. Back before she'd gone to take care of Grandma Ainsley, Isla couldn't remember a day she hadn't been around. She'd taught Isla all about safely exploring and what to do in certain situations, until, eventually, Isla was teaching her what to do. Being raised in this environment had taught her far more than anyone could. Even her mom couldn't approach the animals or blend in with her surroundings like Isla could. But her mother knew all about other things, she remembered, looking up at the sun and back at her friend.

"We'd better head back," she said.

Cash climbed up a root to get out, and Isla followed.

"I can't wait to come back here. It's like our own secret place," Cash said, looking around. "We could even bring snacks and things to do out here." His eyes lit up. "Do you have a pocketknife?"

"Yeah, why?" Isla asked as she handed it to him.

Cash walked up to a tree and removed some bark. Isla watched as he carved his name into it. He handed the pocket-knife to her.

"Your turn," he said with a smile.

Isla grinned. She liked this idea. She carved her name under his. "Now it's *officially* our place," she said as she stood back and looked at it.

The names were a little messy, but they were legible. Isla and Cash both stood there for a few moments, admiring their work, then Isla turned around and started heading back home through the brush. Cash sighed and followed.

"I wish it would clear up again," he said in an annoyed voice.

"This is the fastest way home, and we can't risk being out past sunset," Isla answered.

Cash sped up and walked beside her.

"Has that ever happened before?" he asked nervously.

"Oh yes, but not in a while. Ferdinand used to come and find me when he was younger."

"How long have you had Ferdinand?"

"My dad adopted him as a puppy before I was even born. He's about twelve now."

"Wow, we've never had a dog that long."

"It would be nice to have a dog to explore with, but nowadays all Ferdinand does is lie around."

"You think he'll die soon?" Cash asked.

Isla gulped and turned away from Cash. She didn't like to imagine life without Ferdinand.

"Oh, sorry," Cash apologized.

"It's OK," Isla muttered. She'd never had anyone she loved die. She saw death out on the property all the time, but when she thought about life without Ferdinand's funny little hobble or cute, white-streaked face, her throat and chest got tight, and her eyes stung. She wanted to believe that he'd always be around.

"You think you could teach me how to talk to squirrels?" Cash asked, trying to change the subject.

Isla smiled. "I can try, but it takes patience."

"Good thing we both got a lot of free time," Cash said with a grin.

Suddenly, a strange noise broke through the air. Isla and Cash froze. It sounded like a car beeping.

"What was that?"

"I have no idea," Isla whispered. "I think it came from the neighboring property."

"You don't think it's being developed, do you?"

"I hope not. I'd hate for them to scare all the animals away."

Cash's face lit up. "What if they're building that park we saw?"

Isla frowned. She didn't want a bunch of tourists around.

"I could walk there from my house!" Cash exclaimed.

Isla walked faster. "This place would never be the same if that happened," she said.

"How?" Cash asked.

"The animals would start to disappear. It'd be noisier, and other properties in the area would probably be sold and turned into hotels, restaurants, and stuff like that. The stars would disappear because of all the lights. Coyote County would eventually be completely different," she explained.

"Oh," Cash sighed.

"At least we can explain any weird stuff that goes on."

Cash was quiet a moment. "But what if it isn't being developed?" he asked.

Isla swallowed. That was what was worrying her. "Then something's wrong."

"Bye Isla! I'll see you tomorrow!" Cash shouted as he ran down the road toward his house.

Isla sat on top of the gate and looked up at the sky. They had made it just before dark. Only the very top of the sun could be seen on the horizon. The surrounding sky was different shades of reds, purples, and dark blues. Behind her, she could already see a few stars. The crickets were already chirping, and coyotes were howling up a storm. Sunrise and sunset were the times they hunted. Isla watched as Cash slowly disappeared down the road. She realized that she still wasn't sure where he lived.

A breeze swept through the air. Isla shivered and rubbed her dangling feet together. Her feet were absolutely stained with dirt. Isla sighed as she remembered it was bath night. Lights shined from down the road. Isla watched as a black truck sped down the road toward her.

"Maybe that's what we heard," Isla thought.

She studied the truck and noticed there was mud on the sides. It sped past her down the road toward Cash's house. Isla hoped he was home by now. The driver was going way too fast. She waited and listened for honking or yelling.

After a few minutes, she turned around and hopped off the gate. She smiled when she realized Ferdinand was hobbling toward her.

"Hi, Ferdy!" she shouted.

He wagged his tail and stopped. His head bobbed up and down as he panted. Isla ran to him. She petted him as he slumped against her legs.

She remembered what Cash had said. "I think you're getting a little too old to walk up this road," she said sadly.

Ferdinand's ears perked up when she spoke, and his head turned to the side. Isla got on her knees and gently lifted him across her shoulders. Holding his front paws in her left hand and his back paws in her right, she slowly made her way back home. She was surprised he trusted her enough to let her do this. She could feel his drool easing down her shoulder. She scrunched her nose and tried to ignore it. He was big but not too heavy. His appetite had slowly declined over the months, and he was getting thin.

Isla saw the lights of her house were on and could make out the silhouette of her father's head above the couch. She wondered if he'd already eaten dinner. Her stomach growled at the thought of food. She had only eaten a few acorns at about noon. She looked up at the stars. If the neighboring land did get developed, she feared she'd never see them again. All the lights made it nearly impossible to see them in the city. But you could see thousands of them out here. Isla slowly laid Ferdinand on the ground beside her mom's old car. She took one last look at the sky then walked inside

"Can I drive your truck?" Isla asked her dad after shutting the front door.

Her dad looked up from his book. "What?" he asked as he shifted to a more comfortable position on the couch.

"Can I please drive your truck?" Isla repeated.

"No, I understood you," her father said, staring at her blankly. "But you want to *drive* my truck? Where?"

"Just to the top of the little hill in the meadow. I *think* I could drive it. I've watched you do it so many times."

"Well, that's not very reassuring. Why do you want to drive it?" her dad wanted to know.

"Stargazing." Isla shrugged.

"Tonight?" he exclaimed as he looked at his watch.

"No, just sometime."

"Why don't we go together and I drive?" he asked.

"Because I wanted to go alone, and aren't you busy?" Isla asked.

"I won't be busy this weekend. I'd rather you wait and let me drive," he said.

"Could you at least try to teach me?" she asked hopefully.

He sighed. "I guess so."

"Great! I'll grab the keys!" she exclaimed as she ran off.

"Not tonight! I just got home!" he called to her.

"But you always get home late. If you won't teach me now, you never will!" Isla protested. She peeked her head in the doorway, a hopeful smile on her face.

Her dad sighed and slowly stood up. "OK, let's go."

"Thank you!" Isla cried. She grabbed the keys off a hook on the wall then ran to the front door. Her father opened it, and she bounded down the steps to the truck. Turning around, she saw that he wasn't even down the stairs yet.

"I'm coming. Go ahead and get in the truck," he said.

She turned around and opened the door. It felt strange getting into the driver's seat. The pedals were so far away from her feet. Sitting on the edge of the seat, she reached her feet forward. They just barely touched the pedals. She could see above the steering wheel—enough, anyway. She wasn't going down the highway to the mall. Her dad got in on the passenger side.

"Go ahead and buckle, just in case," her dad said, doing the same.

She quickly got buckled and waited for further instruction.

"First, you need to adjust the seat. There's a handle under the seat in the front. Pull it, and move forward until you can push the brake pedal all the way."

Isla reached forward and pulled the handle. It took all her strength to scooch up, but she figured it out. She reached her left foot forward and pushed the brake all the way.

"No, only your right foot. Don't use both feet when you drive," Christopher told her. "Go ahead and start the truck."

Isla turned the key just like she'd seen him do so many times. The engine roared to life, and Isla grinned, proud of herself. She put her hand on the gearshift. "What do I do with this again?"

"Right now, it's in 'P' for 'park.' Put your foot on the brake, and move it to 'D' for 'drive.'"

"Got it," Isla said.

She did as he said. The truck started to roll forward as soon as she took her foot off the brake.

"Um, Dad," she said, starting to panic.

"You're fine, that's perfectly normal. Now gently press the gas."

Isla slowly pressed the pedal and started driving. It was dark now. Grasshoppers jumped all around in the headlights, trying to get away from the truck. The truck went up and down as it drove over the uneven ground. She slowly turned it as they neared the hill. They got to the top, and she stopped the truck.

"Good! Now keep pressing the brake, and shift the gear to park."

"OK," she said as she did it.

"All right, perfect. Now drive around, and keep doing what I taught you without instructions. "

Isla did so. She loved the feeling of power as she drove her dad's truck. One day, maybe not too far away, she would be able to go wherever she wanted. She drove around the hill a few more times and then drove back to the house and parked the truck.

"You did great," her dad said as they hopped out of the truck.

"So I can drive it now?" she asked.

"Do you feel confident?" he asked as they walked up the steps to the door.

"Yep!" she said.

"Then I guess so, but only if I'm home and the window's open. That way I can hear you if something goes wrong."

"Got it!" Isla said enthusiastically.

She couldn't believe he was actually letting her drive it. Her mom would probably never let her do that. Isla decided not to point that out, in case he changed his mind.

CHAPTER EIGHT

"What are we doing again?" Cash asked.

They were sitting in their place in the woods. Cash sat on a tree root, while Isla sat against the side of the ditch.

She finished chewing her cracker and swallowed. "Stargazing. I'll drive the truck to the best spot, and we'll look at the stars. My mom used to do it with me, and she showed me where all the stars and planets are."

"Oh, OK, that sounds cool. But why do we need the truck?"

Isla shrugged. "When I went with my mom, we always took the truck. We'd either put blankets and pillows in it and lie down or just sit in it. Somehow, it just isn't the same without the truck."

Cash nodded as he stuffed another cracker in his mouth.

"Where did you get these? I've never heard of popcorn-flavored crackers," Isla asked.

Cash shrugged. "My mom found them while she was in town grocery shopping."

"What does your mom do for a living?" Isla asked before eating another cracker.

"She does marketing for some company. What does your dad do?"

"I'm not sure, but it looks real boring," Isla replied.

"So how's your mom and grandma?" Cash asked.

"They're doing pretty good. My mom wants us to visit sometime." She brushed the crumbs off her hands. "What does your little brother do all day?"

"He goes to this special preschool to help with his speech delay. He's been going since we moved here. They think he'll be caught up by the time he starts kindergarten."

"Oh. I thought you just left him at home all day."

Cash gave her a weird look. "My mom would kill me if I did that!"

He dug his hand into his back pocket.

"I brought my iPod," he said as he pulled it out.

Isla jumped up, eager to see this amazing thing he'd told her of. It was bright blue and barely bigger than his hand.

"It's a lot smaller than I imagined," Isla said as she sat next to him.

Cash swallowed his last bite of cracker. "They sell some that are smaller than my thumb."

"Holy cow," Isla muttered as she watched him turn the iPod on.

"These are the apps. You tap on them. See, this one is a camera app."

He tapped on the little app, and the screen completely changed. He pressed a button, and the camera was facing them. Isla jumped a little, startled at suddenly seeing herself. Cash held the iPod above them.

"Smile," he said.

She smiled at the last second, and with just the tap of a finger, the photo was taken. Cash tapped on the photos button to show her it.

"That's awesome, but you need to retake it," she said.

Cash looked at her, confused. "Why?"

"I have a double chin. See?"

Cash laughed, "You look just fine! I didn't even notice!"

"Well, I did. How do you delete it?" She reached for the iPod.

He held the iPod away, still laughing. "It's fine, it's fine!"

"Delete it!" she yelled with a laugh as she crawled over him to grab it.

He took another picture and pulled it away just before she grabbed it.

They both laughed as soon as he went to photos. She and Cash both were making weird faces. She looked crazy, and he looked like he was being crushed.

"OK, you can keep that one. But the other one's gotta go," Isla said before settling on another tree root.

"OK, OK," he said as he deleted it.

She watched as he went back to the page full of apps.

"Do y'all get Wi-Fi out here?" he asked.

"Wi-Fi?"

"Internet connection," Cash tried to explain.

"Maybe at the house, why?"

"I was gonna show you my search on the internet for Forever Innovation, but I need Wi-Fi." He held his iPod up in the air.

Isla smirked at him. "What on earth are you doing?"

"Looking for Wi-Fi!" Cash exclaimed.

"I don't think you're gonna find any all the way out here."

"I'll just show you my games, then."

He scrolled through the apps and tapped one with a robot on it. He shifted the phone in his hands to hold it sideways.

"This is a robot-building game where you make your own custom robot. Then you choose a place to test it out."

He swiped his finger across the screen, and it quickly went across a row of robots. He stopped at a green robot that had lava for hands, rockets for feet, and laser eyes.

"This one's my favorite. I named him Invincible Inferno." He tapped on a picture of a beach.

The game transitioned, and he was playing the robot. Isla watched closely as he flew toward the edge of the water.

"Watch this," he said.

He tapped a button, and lava began shooting at the water's edge. Where the lava met water, it turned into rock.

"Can I try?" Isla asked excitedly.

"Sure," Cash said, handing her the iPod.

She gently took it and copied what he'd done. "How long has this been around?"

"The game or the iPod?" Cash asked.

"Both."

"The iPod's been around for a while, but that game just came out a month ago."

She gently handed the iPod to him. "What else is on it?"

He pressed the home button and looked through the apps again. He tapped on one with a picture of a car.

"This is a racing game. You press the pedal on the screen and tilt it back and forth to steer," he explained while it loaded.

Isla's eyes widened. "It can tell if you tilt it?"

"Yep! Watch," he said as he picked a red race car.

Isla watched as the car moved whichever way Cash moved the iPod. Cash really got into it and was moving his hands so fast, Isla could barely focus on the screen.

"Here, your turn," he said once the race was finished.

Isla tried to do what he did, but she kept running into things. "Good grief! How do you work this thing?" she asked as she tried to get back on the road.

"It takes practice. Let me show you again."

She handed it back to him. He effortlessly won once again.

"You make it look so easy!" Isla exclaimed.

"Because I've played this game so much. Eventually, you'll get it," he reassured her.

Isla looked up through the trees. The sun indicated it was afternoon.

"Oh, I lost track of time! We'd better get going," she said as she jumped up.

Cash stuffed the iPod and empty cracker bag into his pocket. They both stood and began climbing out of the ditch using tree roots.

"Did you ever ask your dad about the trees with those Xes on them?" Cash asked as they trudged on.

"No. I thought about it for hours the night we found them. I figure maybe the old owner put 'em there," Isla replied. "Why?"

"They looked kind of fresh to me. I've used spray paint on my bike before. I know what a fresh coat and an old coat look like."

Isla stopped in her tracks. "Someone put them there *recently*?"

Cash stopped ahead of her and looked back. "Yeah, you should ask your dad about it."

"OK, I will," Isla said, a slight tremble in her voice.

Isla parked the truck so it faced toward the house and so her dad couldn't see the bed from the window. She took out the keys and got out. The moon shined bright on the tall grass and truck. She started climbing into the back, where Cash already was.

Cash's head popped up from the inside. "That was awesome! I've never ridden in the back of a truck before!"

"Really?" Isla asked.

"Yeah, we've never owned one, and I don't think it's legal where I used to live."

"Oh, well, I guess it's legal when you're not on the road."

Cash helped her climb in, and they sat on the giant silver toolbox in the bed of the truck. Isla scooted toward the back of the box and put her feet up in front of her. Cash did the same. He hugged his knees as he looked up.

His mouth fell open. "Whoa," he gasped.

For it wasn't just a few stars, it was the *galaxy*. Isla pointed up at a group of stars with what looked like white and pink dust all around them.

"That's the Milky Way," she said.

He marveled at it all in silent amazement.

"You see that little red star?"

"Yes?"

"That's not a star, that's Jupiter," Isla told him.

"That's Jupiter?" Cash exclaimed. "You can actually see Jupiter from here?"

"Not just Jupiter. You see that almost yellow-looking one?"

"I think so."

"That's Saturn."

"Saturn? This is amazing! In the city, all I could see was maybe a couple stars."

"Out here, there aren't a bunch of lights. That's why you can see so much," she said. "Look at those stars in a line—that's the Little Dipper."

She tried to draw them out with her finger as she pointed.

"Oh, now I see it," he said excitedly.

"And over here is the Big Dipper," she said as she drew it out too.

The two gazed up at the night sky for an hour as Isla pointed out constellations. They even tried to make up their own.

"If you look carefully at the moon, you can see the Man in the Moon," Isla said.

"The Man in the Moon?" Cash said, confused.

"It's a face looking down toward the left, see?"

He stared at it for a few moments. "Oh, I see it now!"

She pointed straight up above them.

"And that bright one, right there, is my star. I claimed it when I was six," Isla said. "I called it my wishing star."

"You see the bright blue one beside yours? I want that one to be my star," Cash said. "That way, even our stars can be best friends."

Isla looked over at him, glad she had thought to share this with him. "I think that's a wonderful idea."

CHAPTER NINE

"*Split up?*" Cash asked, horrified.

It was a sunny, late-June day, and the two were sitting by the big creek that ended in a little pool. The drought was over. The tall, surrounding trees were full of green leaves, and the creek had grown replete from the showers of May. It had a soft current and made a beautiful noise as it ran into the pool. They both had their bare feet resting in the warm waters. Little fish occasionally brushed past their toes. To them, this place was paradise.

"Cash, I've been your guide for about a month now. I think it's time you tried doing it on your own."

"You just want a day with your deer friends," Cash accused her, crossing his arms.

Isla didn't see what was wrong with this. "Why, yes, yes I do."

Cash looked hurt. "Ain't I good enough?" he asked.

"I love hanging out with you, but I haven't been with the deer in a month!" Isla tried to explain. "I just want one afternoon." She gave Cash a pitiful look, and he tried not to look at her.

"Fine, I guess I'll be all right on my own for one afternoon," he agreed finally.

He seemed so disappointed, though, Isla didn't want to leave him just yet, so she sat beside him a little longer, until he stood. He pulled his jeans up to his knees. He walked down the creek and watched a little school of fish jump down the stream. Isla joined him. The cool water felt great in the summer heat. The only regret Isla had about having Cash around was that she couldn't take her clothes off and swim. She had finally asked her dad for a swimsuit, but it was taking a while to come in the mail. So for now, they just got in up to their knees. Even though Cash had a swimsuit, he didn't want to make Isla watch him have all the fun. So he was waiting with her for her swimsuit to come in.

"So does your dad know I exist yet?" he asked randomly as he started walking back.

"Well, no. Not yet, at least."

Cash sighed. "I'd like to be able to go into your house for lunch without constantly looking out the window to see if he's coming. Besides, why are you so afraid to tell him, anyway?"

Isla fiddled with her fingers. "I just don't know how he'd respond."

Cash looked at her levelly. "Does your dad want you to be a loner?"

Isla looked down. "No."

"Does your dad have something against eleven-year-old boys?"

"No."

"Then you've got nothing to worry about!" Cash said as he gently elbowed her in the arm.

"Remember what I told you before? I'm just afraid he won't want you to explore," Isla said.

"Why?" Cash asked.

"Because he'd be responsible for you, and it can be dangerous out here," she explained.

"I'm sure he'll be OK with it. I'll be fine as long as you *stay with me*," he said as he raised an eyebrow.

"It'll only be for maybe an hour!" she said with a laugh. "And OK. I'll tell him tonight."

Cash smiled and stood up. He extended his hand out to help her up.

"I guess I'll see you later, then," he said magnanimously. "If I survive, that is."

Isla laughed and shoved him playfully. "You'll be fine! And if something *does* happen, just scream my name and climb a tree."

Isla hugged him quickly and ran off, leaving him there. She looked back as she ran over the smooth stones near the creek, waving as she left. She was looking forward to seeing the deer. A lot had changed since she'd met Cash. She could talk almost perfectly now, and she got to see Cash six days a week. He was too busy to see her Sunday because he had church and it was his "family day," when he said his whole family went out to eat after church and played games all afternoon. Cash had invited

Isla before, but she was too scared to go just yet. She spent her Sundays trying to catch up on math. She was on summer break now, except for math. Her dad promised that if she could finish the book, she'd be done till the fall.

Isla wondered what would happen with Cash once school started. He would be gone all the time then. She wasn't sure what she'd do without him. She'd forgotten, with her mom gone, what is was like to explore with someone. What was the point of exploring if she had no one to do it with? And, in some ways, hanging out with Cash was even better.

Her steps slowed as she walked away, and Isla started to get a bad feeling in the pit of her stomach. Was she doing the right thing? Cash knew how to survive, but could he really find his way around? She shoved the thoughts away. He'd learned a lot. He was plenty smart enough to be on his own.

She crouched down and quietly moved a few leaves off the ground to reveal a hoofprint pointing north. The deer had moved since she last saw them, so it could be a while before she found them. A welcoming breeze swept through her hair as she stood up. Her neck was always sweaty from her hair these days. Sometimes she just wanted to chop it all off. But her hair was now over two feet long, and she knew it would take forever to get it back to that length. She continued on the path and listened to the birds. Suddenly she heard a familiar noise.

Ruckus, she thought, identifying the rattlesnake's warning. She was surprisingly happy that he still nested under the dead tree lying on the ground near Piper. She wondered if he still respected her. Changing her course slightly, she headed toward the tree to see him. The old tree now had mushrooms on it and was probably filled with ants by now. Vines girdled it from top to bottom. The tall weeds made it hard to see underneath, but Isla soon spotted his rattle. Near the tree was some old snakeskin. Ruckus was getting old. It made her sad, somehow. When he was gone, she'd miss that special noise of his.

She decided to leave the now-annoyed Ruckus and continue toward the deer. Hoofprints soon became clearer, and the deer came into view. Isla smiled and began to approach them. She walked toward the edge of a steep hill. Stepping onto the edge, little rocks slid down. She jumped back, afraid of sliding off. The hill had a sudden drop, about five feet long, and then sloped down. It was covered in brown and white rocks both big and small. She grabbed a thick vine, tested its strength, and then slowly made her way down the drop. For some, this would be a simple task. But for her, it was a long ways down. She slowly lowered herself onto the ground. The rest didn't seem too difficult. This part of the hill wasn't nearly as steep, but it had its own dangers. The bottom of the hill was rockier, and some of the rocks were sharp and jagged. It was very uncomfortable on her feet, and she had to be very cautious. Each rock had to be tested before she stepped on it. If a rock were loose, she could easily fall and get injured. The sun beat down on her as she slowly made her way down the hill. Not a single cloud could be seen in the blue, sunny sky. But there the deer were in a meadow not too far away.

Just then, a rat snake slithered through the rocks below her. Isla steadied herself with a mesquite tree as she watched the snake chase a mouse. A chill ran down her spine as she realized that it had been right under her and she hadn't noticed it.

These days, sometimes she and Cash made enough noise that animals often ran before she was that close. "I have got to work on my awareness," Isla mumbled as she stepped onto another rock. Usually she knew if snakes were around her.

But, startled by the snake, Isla had forgotten to test her weight. The rock she stood on slipped out from underneath her, and she went with it. Her arms flung forward, trying to find a hold or keep her from hitting her head. The world spun around her, and she hated it. She couldn't tell what was up and what was down as she tumbled. Her head hit something hard, and everything went black.

Isla's eyes fluttered open. The familiar smell of smoke burned her nose. Something warm and wet was running down her forehead. She was moving up and down—someone was carrying her. Her head throbbed as she tried to make sense of what she was seeing. It was Cash. He was carrying her through the woods. He looked distressed: his face was flushed, and he was breathing very hard. She slowly lifted her eyes past his head. There was a cloud of smoke rising in the air. She couldn't make heads or tails of what was going on. She looked at his shirt and saw a large patch of blood on it. The confusion just made her head throb even more. She let out a groan.

"It's OK, Isla, I'll get you help," Cash said in a trembling voice.

"Help?" Isla murmured. What was going on? Why did she need help? Unfortunately, she didn't have time to try and figure it out, as the world spun around her, and she lost consciousness again.

Isla slowly opened her bleary brown eyes and tried to adjust to the brightness of the room. She slowly scanned the walls, trying to figure out where she was. There was a picture of a gorilla, there was a hand-washing station, and she soon found an IV in her left hand. She let out an exasperated sigh as she realized that this was, in fact, a hospital. Her head felt uncomfortably concealed. She slowly raised her arm to feel it. There was a cloth-like material wrapped around her forehead. She looked at her hospital gown and wondered what had happened to her clothes. They were so worn out that Isla wondered if the nurses had thrown them away.

A snore rang out from across the room. Startled, she looked up to see her dad sitting in a chair. His head was lying against the wall, and his neck was so far back that Isla was sure he'd end up with a crick in it. His green-and-black Western shirt's sleeves were folded back toward his elbows. He was always forgetting to unroll them after washing his hands. His Bible was lying open in his lap with his glasses lying on top of it.

Isla looked up at the TV. There was a cartoon show on with a kid whose head was shaped like a Dorito. She wasn't so sure what was going on because someone had muted it. She hadn't seen a cartoon in years. She thought cartoons consisted of foolish animals and classical music. This was not at all that.

"Oh, Isla, you're awake! How do you feel?" her dad asked groggily as he stood up and walked to the bedside.

"What happened?" Isla slowly asked.

"A neighbor called me saying that she had spotted smoke over our property and called 911."

"Oh," Isla said as she sadly gazed down at the bed sheets.

"She also said that her son was missing, and he ended up being on our property," her dad said, raising his left eyebrow.

"Oh!" Isla said. She started nervously fiddling with her fingers. "So, how's her son?" she asked.

"Better than you are," her dad said pointedly. He folded his arms. "So. How long has Cashton been hanging out on the property?"

"Oh, I don't know, a little while," Isla hedged, trying to avoid eye contact.

"You're not in trouble, Isla. I'm happy you've made a friend. I just wonder why you didn't tell me," her dad said.

"I wasn't sure how you'd react. Nothing like this had ever happened before," Isla said as she slowly looked up at him.

Her dad looked hard at her and then sighed. "I wondered what was going on," he admitted. "You've been so much happier. Is he the reason why you're doing so much better talking?"

"I think so," Isla said shyly. "He says it's probably somethin' that gets better with practice." After so long, it was good to tell her father about her friend, especially since he wasn't mad.

Christopher laughed. "That's true," he said. "Well. Cashton sure made a swell first impression." He put his hands in his pockets and leaned back.

"What do you mean?" Isla asked nervously. She couldn't tell if he was being serious or sarcastic.

Her dad looked at her, very serious. "Isla, when Cashton saw the fire, he ran to find you. He carried you about half a mile away from the blaze. Had to put you down at the barbed-wire fence, but he ran all the way to the house to get the fire trucks to tell them where you were. Soot-faced kid, blood all over his shirt, absolutely tuckered out—I was worried to death about you, and I could've sworn he was an angel. He saved your life."

"Really?" Isla asked as she started to smile. She tried to stop, but it was one of those smiles that you simply just can't control.

"Really," her dad replied.

Isla imagined him carrying her through the woods while escaping a roaring fire. But her smile soon turned into a frown as she began to think about the fire.

"What was the cause of the fire?" she asked.

Her dad sighed and shifted from side to side. "The police suspect arson," he admitted.

CHAPTER TEN

"Arson?" Isla asked.

"They think the fire was set on purpose," her dad explained.

"*On purpose*?" Isla exclaimed as her head shot up. "They think someone trespassed and set it *on purpose*?"

Her dad nodded. "To make things worse, they set it near you."

"What do you mean?"

"The police say there's a possibility that they were targeting you."

Isla didn't understand. "Why? I don't know no one that wants to hurt me!"

Her dad rubbed a hand on the back of his head. "We thought the first fire was just the drought and an accident, but after the rain we had last month, the police suspected foul play and tested the debris. They found traces of kerosene."

"What's kerosene?"

"It's an accelerant commonly used to start fires."

"What's an accelerant?'

"Something used to help start fires."

"Oh," Isla said as she nervously gulped. "Is there any chance that it could have already been there for some time?"

"I doubt that. Somebody would have had to ignite it."

"What does ignite mean?"

Christopher patted her knee. "OK, how about you rest awhile," he said.

"But I just *got* to know more!" Isla protested as her father kissed her forehead.

"There will be time for that, but right now you need to rest," he said.

He sat back down and opened his Bible. Isla sighed and hunkered down into the bed. But her mind was racing, and there was no way she could fall asleep. Not after waking to find herself hurt in the hospital after a fire had been set on their property—on purpose! It was hard to take in, especially because she had learned in a matter of minutes that all of this had happened.

"So when do we leave?" she said a few moments later.

Her dad had just put his glasses back on and was reading the Bible.

"When the doctor comes back in."

"When will the doctor come back in?"

"Shhhh." He looked back at the Bible. Isla bit her lip and winced. She lay back down and stared at the ceiling. Her vision was a little off. Every once in a while, a wave of color would sort of appear in the corner of her eyes. But as soon as she looked at it directly, it would disappear. She also felt sort of bubbly. She looked at the packet that held whatever medicine was streaming into her hand, but the words were too small to read. She figured it was the source of this funny feeling. She was strangely tempted to growl at it but figured it'd be better to stay quiet.

After a while, though, someone knocked on the door. Isla and her father both sat up at the same time to see two familiar faces. It was Darrel and Carroll, the elderly couple from the wedding. Isla was surprised at how happy she was to see them. Once again, she found herself smiling uncontrollably as her father stood up to greet them.

"We came as soon as we heard the news! Oh, how are you, darling?" Carroll asked in a concerned voice as she walked to Isla's bedside.

"I've been better," Isla admitted.

Carroll brushed Isla's hair off of the bandage.

"You poor thing! What happened? Did you get stitches?" Carroll asked.

She gently took Isla's right hand. Isla looked at her dad for an answer. She wasn't really sure what had happened, herself.

"Only three," her dad said as he and Darrel walked up to the bed.

"Please tell me you at least got an ice cream cone out of it," Darrel said as he looked at her forehead.

Isla shook her head and looked at her dad. Darrel punched Christopher in the arm.

"Oh, Christopher, surely you planned on getting her ice cream!"

Her dad smiled and protested, "I was too focused on getting to the hospital to think about ice cream."

"Don't worry, hon, I'll make sure you get a big scoop of it!" Darrel promised her.

"A balloon too!" Carroll added.

Isla grinned slowly. She loved this newfound attention. Her dad had some pretty awesome people working for him. Once again she thought how much Darrel and Carroll reminded her of the grandparents she wished she'd had. She'd never known a full set, just Grandma Ainsley, and she lived all the way in Scotland. Darrel's phone buzzed, and he put on his reading glasses. He squinted at the text message, and his mouth moved to the words as he read it in his head.

"Robert and Alexander just left work. They're on their way to the hospital," Darrel said as he put the phone back in his shirt pocket.

"Oh, OK. We met Robert at his wedding, and I believe you met Alexander too," her dad reminded Isla.

"Yeah, he was the one who shared his dessert with me!" Isla exclaimed.

"I'm going to ask him to bring you the goodies," Darrel said as he squinted at his phone and slowly typed it in.

"Thank you!" Isla said.

"Here, let me fix your pillows so that you can sit up better!" Carroll offered kindly.

She gently put her hand on Isla's back and pushed her forward. She fluffed the pillows and put them on top of each other. Isla slowly leaned back into the wonderful plushness of the white pillows, trying to remember the last time she had felt so comfortable and looked after.

Carroll started to play with Isla's hair, teasing out the tangles. "So what exactly happened?"

Isla got a chill. She loved it when people played with her hair. "Well, I was climbing down a rocky hill by myself when suddenly, I slipped, and a rock knocked me out." Isla paused for Carroll's gasp. "Then my friend Cash found me and carried me through the woods to save me from the fire."

Carroll shook her head. "Oh honey, you poor thing!"

Darrel was more interested in another part of the story. He raised his eyebrows. "Wait, so a *boy* saved you?"

Isla smiled and scrunched her nose. "We're just friends," she said quickly. She saw where this was going.

"Your mouth tells one tale, but that smile tells another!" Darrel said with a laugh.

"We really are just friends," Isla protested.

"Oh, I'm just teasing you!" Darrel said, patting her knee. "You're not even interested in boys, are you?"

"Well, er, I um . . ." Isla said, trying to figure out how to respond.

Her dad looked up sharply. "No boys till you're thirty!"

Isla gave him a look, as if to say, "Seriously?"

Another knock sounded at the door. Isla looked up, delighted, at her other two visitors: Robert from the wedding and Alexander, with two balloons that read "Get Well Soon" and a stuffed red bear with a red ribbon tied around its neck. After the wedding, it was a little strange seeing both men in such casual clothes—everyone in the room had blue jeans and comfy shirts on.

"Hey! How's it going, squirt?" Alexander asked as he headed toward the bed.

"I'm feeling a lot better now!" Isla replied as he handed her the bear. "Thanks!"

"You're welcome. You should name it Alexander," he suggested as Isla stroked the bear's fur.

"If anything, she'll name it Robert!" Robert joked, walking up to the end of the bed. "I'm the one who ran into the store to get it for you!"

"Thank you too, Robert," Isla said shyly. "I can't believe all of y'all came to visit me."

"Of course we came," Darrel said. "Getting rushed to the emergency room is a very serious thing. We all wanted to make sure you were all right."

Isla smiled, and her eyes began to water. She felt as if she might cry. She hadn't felt lonely before the wedding and meeting Cash—she'd had her parents and Ferdy and the animals and thought she was just fine. She hadn't known how much she'd been missing. There were so many good people in the world.

"So, how did you get away from the fire?" Alexander said. He seemed fixated on her forehead. Really worried.

"My friend carried me to safety."

"I thought you didn't have any friends out there," he said, confused.

"What made you think that?" Isla said, looking up from the bear.

"Well, when your dad talks about you, he never mentions friends, except for the animals, of course."

"That's because Dad didn't know," her dad said. Isla gave him a guilty smile.

"I bet you don't want to stay in those woods anymore, do you?" Alexander said jokingly.

Isla stared at him, bewildered. "Ain't nothin' going to keep me out of those woods!" she said emphatically.

Alexander's phone rang, and he looked a little upset.

"I'm sorry; I need to take this," he said as he walked out of the room.

"So when can we break you out of here?" Robert asked as he took Alexander's place on the right side of the bed.

Isla shrugged. "When the doctor gives the OK, I guess."

"Well, we're gonna get you out of here and into town for some froyo in just a minute, OK?" Robert said.

"Works for me!" Isla exclaimed.

She couldn't tell if it was Cash or the drugs, but she wasn't nearly as shy as she normally was. In fact, all she wanted to do was talk. The doctor came in and looked surprised to see so many people. He had gray hair that swooped up as if a cow had licked him, glasses, and wore one of those white robe-like things that had all the pockets. Isla had always wanted one of those because it had so much storage. She could fit every portable thing she owned in a coat like that. She stared longingly at his coat as he walked in.

"I just need her father to sign a few papers," he said, trying to find a way to Christopher with so many people in the room.

Her dad stepped forward and took them. A nurse opened the door. She had a bag with her. Isla smiled as she realized it must be her clothes.

"There is some blood on them, but we have a nightgown that she could go home in," the nurse said to Isla's dad. "Are you sure you don't want us to throw them away? They're torn all over."

"It's OK, they were already like that," Isla told her. She reached out, wishing to hold her beloved clothes.

"Thank you, the gown will work," her dad told the nurse as she handed the gown and bag to him.

Isla looked at him, confused. "Gown? But my clothes are right there."

"Isla, I am not about to take you home in bloody clothes," her dad said.

"Why not? At least I know it's my blood." She put her hand over the side of her mouth so the doctor couldn't see what she was saying and whispered, "Someone else's blood could have been all over that thing."

"Isla, I'm sure it's perfectly clean," her dad said.

"Don't worry, the gown has just been opened," the doctor reassured her.

Isla stared at his hair. "You been around cows lately?" As if her dad knew where she was going with that question, he hushed her before she could continue.

"I don't think I've ever heard you talk this much," he laughed.

Isla pointed to the medicine. "I think it's because of whatever's in that thing."

"Yes, we gave you some pretty strong pain medicine," the doctor said with a smile.

Her dad finished the paperwork and handed it to the doctor.

Meanwhile, Carroll had been examining the clothes in her bag. "Oh darling, these clothes are just so old and worn out! Let me take you shopping!" she said, horrified.

"Er, ah, thanks, but no thanks! I'm quite attached to those."

"Oh, come on, every girl loves a little shopping!" Carroll persisted.

Isla shook her head. "Well, I'm not exactly like every girl."

"You know, I used to be a little wild, just like you! Now look at me, wearing nice clothes and broaches. You grow to love it!"

Isla eyed Carroll's stiff hair, full of hairspray, her makeup, fancy purple shirt, long black pants, and pretty purple sandals. She was so beautiful, but it wasn't exactly how Isla imagined her future self.

"Isla would love to. You can take her tomorrow around noon," Isla's dad said.

"Excuse me?" Isla said, giving her dad a confused look.

"I was planning on taking her to work anyway. You can pick her up at our house then bring her by the office afterwards," her dad told Carroll as Alexander walked back in.

"What did I miss?" he asked.

"I'm taking Isla shopping!" Carroll said happily.

She just seemed so excited. Isla gave Alexander a look that said, "Help!" Alexander looked at her and winked. "Are you sure? Tomorrow is Saturday, and the stores will be packed," he said to Carroll.

"Oh, nonsense! A few extra people won't harm anything!"

"Sorry, squirt, I tried!" Alexander told Isla.

"Thanks," Isla said glumly. She sighed. She remembered the last time she'd gone shopping. If there had been a lot of people staring at her before she had the big bandage on her forehead, how bad would it be now?

"We'll wait for you in the hall while you change," Darrel said as he, Carroll, Robert, and Alexander started to leave.

The nurse brought in a blue nightgown for Isla to wear until she got home. She carefully removed the IV in Isla's hand. "Well, at least you'll have a great story to tell when school starts up again," the lady said as she put the IV up.

"I'm homeschooled."

"Oh, well, then you'll have a great story to tell your family," the nurse decided.

Isla hadn't thought about that. She groaned. Her mother would never let her set foot into the woods when she heard this! The lady walked out of the room, and Isla's dad handed her the gown.

"Can we keep this a secret from Mom?" Isla asked him, taking the blue gown and unfolding it.

Her dad was not impressed. "Now, why would you want to do that?"

"She might not let me explore anymore if she finds out that someone might have tried to murder me out there."

"Well, I already talked to her on the phone. She would have talked to you, but you were still asleep," her dad sighed. "We've *both* agreed that you should stay around the house or with me until things settle down."

"What! But what if things *never* settle down?"

"Don't worry, I'm sure the police have their best investigators tracking down the arsonists as we speak," her dad promised her. He helped her stand and started to untie the knots in the back of Isla's hospital gown. "Can you move your hair out of the way?"

She moved her hair onto her shoulder. "What if they burn the house down? Then what do we do?"

"If they make a bold move like that, we'll catch 'em," her dad replied.

Isla quickly slipped on the blue gown. She pulled at the gown, trying to stretch it out. She was used to wearing big clothes.

"Don't forget to remind me that we need to clean the stitches twice a day," Isla's dad said.

"Does that mean I'll need a shower every night?"

"Yep," he said as he grabbed her hand and led her to the door.

"Great," Isla moaned.

They walked down the wide halls. A couple of people were being pushed around in wheelchairs. A moan of pain could be heard in the distance. Doctors and nurses rushed all around. Isla couldn't believe she was actually here. It seemed like just moments ago she was exploring on the property, and now she didn't know when she'd be allowed out there again. As they approached the doors to leave, Isla was shocked to see that the sun had already gone down.

"How long have we been here?" she asked.

"A few hours. It took you a little while to wake up," he said as they walked across the street.

"Where's Cash?"

"He left over an hour ago. He wanted to stay and wait for you to wake up, but his mom needed to get home," her dad explained.

He opened the truck door for her. She got in, and then he got in on his side. He pulled out his phone.

"Since when do you have a smartphone?" Isla asked.

"I've had this one for a long time. You probably haven't seen it because I rarely use it." He dialed her mom's number. "Here, your mom's been waiting to talk to you."

Isla slowly took the phone and held it up to her ear. She wasn't sure if she could press the screen against her face, so she just barely held it away. The phone rang maybe four times before there was finally an answer.

"Hello!" a voice suddenly spoke. "Isla, are you there?"

She froze when she heard her mom's voice. She hadn't heard it in so long. The emotion from the whole ordeal suddenly hit her.

"Yes, I'm here," she said, starting to cry.

Her dad laid his hand on her shoulder.

"Are you OK?" Her mom asked. She sounded so worried, even scared.

Isla swallowed and wiped her eyes. She didn't want to scare her mom. "Yes, I'm OK," she said. "Mom, they suspect arson!"

"I know," her mom breathed heavily. It sounded as if she was fixing to cry too.

"But can I keep exploring if I'm real careful?" Isla asked, a little shakily.

There was a pause on the line.

"Isla, it's too dangerous. I want you to stay with your father until these people are caught," her mom told her.

Isla slumped in her seat. "OK," she muttered, a little reluctantly.

"I'm coming down there as soon as I can!" her mom promised.

Isla felt guilty. Her Grandma Ainsley was really sick. "You don't have to, I'm really OK."

"No, Isla, I *need* to come back. I need to see you and be with you and your father during this time."

"What about Grandma Ainsley?" Isla asked.

"A family friend is staying with her. I couldn't book two tickets," her mom explained. "I won't be there for a few days, but I'm coming."

Isla admitted she wanted her mom in the middle of all of this. "OK, Mom. I can't wait to see you."

"And I can't wait to see you. I have to go. I love you, Isla!"

"I love you too, Mom!"

She slowly pulled the phone away from her ear as it hung up. She sniffled as she handed it back to her dad.

CHAPTER ELEVEN

Isla lay in bed, debating whether or not to get up. She could see the sun had just barely risen over the hills. Usually she'd already be up and out the door, excited to meet up with Cash. But today she was going shopping. She wished she could find a way out of it. Her head was pretty sore, but that probably wasn't a good enough excuse.

"If only I had broken a leg. Then I couldn't go," she mumbled as she turned onto her side.

She looked at the golden-colored handle on her door. Her white dress was hanging on it. It was all she had to wear until her shirt and jeans got washed. Her eyes drifted around the room until she saw a picture that got her attention. It was a picture of her sitting on her mom's lap on a log by a creek, the first time she'd ever been exploring. Her mom had short, dark-brown hair and had a fuzzy blue hat, a blue scarf, a gray sweater, brown boots, and jeans on. Isla was about three years old and wore an exact replica of her mom's outfit, except it was all pink. Her mom smiled at the camera while Isla looked down at something in her hands.

She closed her eyes and tried to remember that day.

It was a cold day in October. The trees were almost completely stripped of their leaves. Their branches brushed against one another in the wind, making lovely, creepy noises as they touched. Isla held a cold lizard she'd found next to a rock, too cold to move.

Isla loved animals, and she was determined to keep the poor thing warm. It gazed up at her as she held it in her favorite pink gloves. She heard her dad say, "Cheese!" but she was too intrigued by the lizard to look up.

"Momma, are dere more aminals in the foest?" she asked.

"Oh yes, there are lots and lots of animals all over the forest! Would you like to see them all?" her mom asked as she looked down at the lizard in little Isla's hands.

Isla nodded.

"It'll be hard, but if you're real quiet and come out here often with me, we just might eventually see every one of them!"

Isla smiled, and her mom set her down on the ground.

They hadn't seen any more animals that day, Isla remembered, staring at the photo. But as the years went by, Isla had become acquainted with hundreds of animals. First small ones, but when Isla had started exploring on her own at six years old, she'd gotten to know the coyotes, bobcats, hawks, and deer. At first, she'd been too scared to go ten feet past the broken barbed wire. But as time went on, she soon got braver and ventured off further.

She'd spent so much of her short life in the woods watching the animals. She hadn't been too old before she'd learned to mimic their cries and act like they did. She'd learned how to approach the deer when she was eight. It had taken months for her to do it right. Her time in the forest had taught her patience, gentleness, bravery, and self-control. She hadn't given her parents much trouble growing up. They'd encouraged her wandering until now.

But now, her wild side was calling her away. "Isla! Breakfast!" her dad called.

Isla slowly got out of bed. She took one last look at the picture, then walked down the hall to the kitchen. She walked in just as her dad pulled biscuits out of the oven. Seeing him wearing her mom's colorful apron and matching oven mitts made Isla giggle a little. His glasses were on the edge of his nose, just about to fall off. It bothered her when he didn't fix them.

"You can make biscuits?" Isla asked.

"Your mom taught me how. I just didn't decide to try until this morning. Let's just hope they're edible," her dad said with a chuckle.

Isla grabbed a stick of butter from their gray refrigerator and a knife from a drawer. Her dad put the biscuits on the table and laid out plates.

"Do you want to keep that gown from the hospital?" her dad asked as he sat down. Isla sat and looked down at the gown. She had forgotten she was wearing it.

"I don't know. It reminds me of the hospital," Isla said, sniffing the sleeve doubtfully. She could almost still smell the antiseptic and the sick people.

"If you don't want it, you can throw it away," her dad said as he buttered his biscuits. "Are you ready to go shopping with Carroll?"

"I guess so," Isla said reluctantly.

"Trust me, shopping with another woman will be so much more fun than shopping with me," her dad said with a smile.

"Another woman! *I'm* not a woman yet," Isla protested. Her dad started to eat his biscuits. "Can I start exploring again tomorrow?" Isla asked.

Her dad sighed. "We've been over this, Isla. Not till it's safe." Isla groaned, "What will I do until then?"

"You'll stick with me. I'm sure you'll find something to do."

Isla gazed down at her biscuit. She wasn't very hungry, but she starting eating anyway. She swallowed her first bite and looked up at her dad. "Hey, Dad?"

"Yes?" he said.

"Have you ever painted Xes on the trees?"

"Xes? No, why?"

"I was just curious," she said. It had occurred to her that the people who had painted the trees and dropped the disc could be working with the arsonist, but she didn't want to tell her dad about everything she had found and make him worry even more. Then he'd never let her go back out there.

Ferdinand started to bark, which was quite rare. "That must be Carroll!" her dad said. He stood up and headed toward the front door. Isla shoved the rest of her biscuit into her mouth and forced it down. She ran to her room to get ready. Her white flip-flops were collecting dust under her bed. They hadn't been worn in at least a month. She quickly changed and started brushing her knotted hair. She had to be especially gentle because of her head.

"Aw, nuts," she groaned as she looked at her tan lines.

Her shoulders were so white compared to her tan arms. She laughed when she saw her feet. It looked like she was wearing tan socks because she'd been wearing jeans and no shoes.

"Isla, dear! Are you ready?" Carroll shouted from the living room.

"Yes!" she shouted back. Carroll was especially dressed up today. She wore a red shirt with an inch-long, lizard-shaped broach, black pants, big red earrings, and nice red shoes.

"Good night! You look beautiful!" Carroll exclaimed.

Isla blushed but was confused at the same time. Good night? What on earth did that mean? It wasn't even nighttime.

"So, what's the plan?" her dad asked Carroll.

"Well, we are going to the mall, then we'll grab a bite, then I guess I'll take her to the office."

Isla wrinkled her nose, realizing that she still didn't know exactly where her dad worked or what he did. All she knew was that he was successful.

"We should be heading out," Carroll said as she started walking toward the door.

Isla hugged her dad tight before following. She was starting to get that butterfly feeling in her stomach and regretted eating that biscuit. Climbing into Carroll's tiny red car, she looked past the barbed wire, wishing that she could go through it and into the woods. That was where she belonged, not *shopping*.

Isla sighed as she tried on another shirt. There were clothes all over the small dressing room. Carroll had insisted she use the dressing room so she could see how everything looked, and Isla felt as if she had tried on everything in the whole store. But Carroll was having so much fun finding her clothes, so Isla hadn't begged to leave. They had already found ten shirts, four pairs of jeans, two pairs of pajamas, and a hoodie. Carroll didn't see much point in having a hoodie now, but it was the one thing out of everything they'd found that Isla could see herself wearing. She loved that hoodie. It was black, and the front read, "I'm a Little Wild."

Isla walked out of the dressing room. Carroll gasped, "You look adorable!"

This shirt was light blue with a dark-blue Boston Terrier puppy on the front that covered half of the shirt. On the puppy was a real black bow.

"Is that all?" Isla asked hopefully.

"Yes, it's about lunchtime," Carroll said. She picked up her purse and grabbed the cart. Isla quickly put her dress back on and, carrying the shirt, followed Carroll. This trip to the mall hadn't been *so* bad, she thought. This time, people had only stared at her head. As Carroll paid for the clothes, Isla walked toward the entrance and looked around. She still couldn't believe how clean the mall looked. Looking down at the first story, she saw the cart of rabbits and other rodents. The poor rabbits were in a cage far too small. They were away from their home in the woods, just like she was. Isla smiled dreamily, imagining letting them go. And why shouldn't she?

She slowly looked back to see if Carroll was paying any attention to her. Carroll was slowly handing the cashier change. Isla bit her lip and thought for a moment.

"Should I?" she whispered.

The rabbits looked like they could use a bit of freedom. Her hands twitched as she wavered back and forth. Then she remembered Sammy, Acorn, and Piper. They were so happy being free, wouldn't a couple spotted bunnies be happy too? Isla couldn't help herself.

She darted to the escalator, walking down the steps to get down faster, hoping Carroll hadn't noticed, and assessing the situation. The man working at the cart was talking to a customer on the opposite side, two bunnies were closest to Isla, the security guard was about twenty feet away, and there weren't many people walking around.

Stepping off the escalator, she looked both ways. Nobody was watching. She took a deep breath and quickly walked up to the cart. She picked up the small cage and set it on the floor. Then, without hesitation, she opened the door and gently pulled the rabbits out. Once free, they bolted into a crowd of people. For a moment, time seemed to go in slow motion as she processed what was happening. The man who worked the cart was yelling and gesticulating his arms as if a snake had crawled up his pants. People screamed as rabbits ran past their feet, and children were laughing and pointing. A person came into view in Isla's peripheral vision—a person that was running right toward her.

Suddenly, reality hit her. It was the security guard! Isla dodged his outstretched arms and pelted off after the rabbits. Running, she made the high-pitched noise she used to call both squirrels and rabbits. Surprisingly, it worked, and the rabbits followed.

Isla laughed at the sheer joy of it. She'd never felt so alive. She dodged kids and adults, jumping over boxes and carts in her way, just ahead of the angry security guard. She neared the door and opened it wide. The rabbits bounded outside and into the nearest bushes. Isla beamed, elated. For a moment, everything was so exciting and great. Then, that moment ended.

"You did *what!*"

It was a few hours later. After a load of paperwork, a few payments, a lecture from a much-flustered Carroll, and the longest car ride Isla had ever been in, they were finally at her dad's office, and he wasn't very happy.

"Why on earth would you think that it would be all right to set rabbits free from a *store!*"

Isla squirmed. "I couldn't help it. Those big brown eyes were taunting me, *begging* me to help them," she explained.

She looked up at her dad hopefully, but quickly looked back down when she saw the expression on his face. Her dad let out a frustrated sigh. "We will talk about this later," he said sternly. "For now, you need to apologize to Carroll."

Isla felt genuinely guilty as she looked up at the nice, grandmotherly lady. "I'm sorry, Carroll," she said.

Carroll regarded her for a moment, then sighed and hugged Isla. "Oh, I can't stay mad at that face. Just don't do it again," she said.

"I won't," Isla promised as Darrel walked in.

"You ready for the big tour?" he asked Isla.

Isla nodded, and they walked out of the little office. Along with how to upset a mall security guard, today she had learned that apparently her dad owned an oil well. She wasn't too sure what that was or how it made any money, but she was about to find out. So far, it didn't seem like much. They were in an outdated, two-story building in an old town.

Isla followed along after Darrel, but she couldn't pay much attention to what he was saying. She was looking for Alexander. He'd been so nice at the wedding and the hospital. If he was like a brother to her father, maybe he could be her fun uncle. Walking down the old halls, she peeked into every office. They made a right turn and walked down a shorter hallway with only three doors. The first door read "Meeting Room." Darrel opened the door to reveal a room with a long table, many chairs that spun around, a whiteboard, a TV, and four men who appeared to be talking about a decision for the company. Isla immediately spotted Alexander sitting toward the end of the table. He looked up and smiled.

"How's that head of yours, squirt?" he asked as they walked in.

Isla beamed and ran up to him. "It's all right." She sat down next to him, her dad sat beside her, and Carroll and Darrel sat on the other side of the table.

"Here, take this before we bore you to death," Alexander said.

He handed her his smartphone, which was rather large. It made Cash's iPod and her dad's phone look puny. The screen looked far more expensive too. Isla gently took it, afraid that she might break it. She had never held something so expensive looking.

"Thanks, how do I turn it on?" she asked, puzzled.

Alexander looked shocked to hear those words come out of her mouth. He took the phone and turned it on. He swiped through the apps and chose one.

"Touch the screen to play the game. If you need help, there is a question mark in the corner that will explain everything."

Isla held the phone in her hands as gently as if she were holding one of Piper's babies and slightly tapped the play button on the screen. The meeting commenced, but she hardly even noticed. She was too absorbed in the game. The object of the game was to run from these weird monkey-like creatures. At first, she failed miserably, but within a few minutes, she had it figured out. Rapidly swiping her finger, she was no longer gentle. The phone was far sturdier than she'd thought. But to her dismay, she accidentally hit the home button.

She looked up at Alexander, but he was too busy talking. Isla carefully slid her finger through the pages of apps and tried to do what he had done. Scrolling through pages, she was shocked to find that he had five pages full of apps. She sighed and looked at each one carefully. Suddenly, the phone vibrated, and a notification appeared at the top. It was a text.

It read, "Isn't that what you wanted?"

Alexander quickly took the phone from her to look at it. Surprised, Isla jumped and wondered what was so important about it. Apparently, everyone else was confused, too, because when she looked up, they had all stopped talking and were looking at Alexander.

"Sorry about that, squirt, my friend texted me," he apologized, looking embarrassed.

He went back into the app and handed her the phone. Isla warily took it back, afraid that it would vibrate and he'd snatch it up again. The meeting continued as Isla started trying to beat Alexander's high score again.

CHAPTER TWELVE

Isla sat in bed, stroking the fur of the red teddy bear she had received while in the hospital. The moon shined bright through her open window, and crickets were the only things that could be heard. It was around midnight, and there was no way that Isla was falling asleep. So much had happened today. She'd shopped for hours, she'd released the bunnies, she'd visited her dad's work, and she'd gotten to see Alexander and his magical phone.

Out the window, the property seemed endless. Sniffling, she put the bear down and walked over to her window. The moon was so bright that tonight she wouldn't need a flashlight to see everything. Isla drummed her fingers on the windowsill. She'd done so many fun things today, but at the day's end, she craved the outdoors more than ever. Her heart raced as she imagined herself climbing out the window and exploring. It wouldn't be the first time she had done so, but she'd never done it with the chance of running into an arsonist—or against her parents' express orders.

The itch was too strong to ignore. She couldn't take it anymore. Running across the room, she grabbed a T-shirt and a pair of jeans. She threw them on, grabbed her pocketknife, and carefully crawled out the window. She had never felt so wonderful as she ran through the tall, moonlit grass and headed toward the barbed wire. Crawling through the barbed wire, she quickly set off into the woods. Once far away from the house, she climbed a tree. Everything looked amazing in the moonlight. Isla felt as if she were in a movie. At the top of the tree, she threw her head back on a whim and howled at the top of her lungs. All was quiet, and Isla froze, listening for a response. Then a pack of coyotes took up the cry. Isla smiled and squealed with excitement. She joined them again and continued to howl with them until they grew quiet. A shiver ran down her spine. Just a few hours ago, she'd thought she'd never get to do that ever again.

Her thoughts turned to her friend. "I hope Cash doesn't think I'm ignoring him," she murmured.

She hadn't been home all day and hadn't talked to him since before they went to the hospital. She slowly climbed down the tree as she tried to remember which direction Cash always came from. She had never been to his house before. As soon as she hit the ground, she started running toward the gate. She figured that she would find his house and tell him everything that had happened, and then they would have some fun. As she ran, she was constantly looking left and right. The arsonist could be around. It was scary to think about, but also exciting. And she didn't plan on going to the hospital again. She slowed down as she neared the gate. Cautiously looking left and right down the old road, she slowly climbed over the gate. She tried to stay in the shadows as she started down the road. The one thing she feared more than anything was strangers. If a passing car saw her, she could end up in trouble with her dad or kidnapped. Once again, she thought of the pale man in the store.

Isla gulped. If Cash could come to her house every day, couldn't she go to his? A house came into view, and her heart gave a leap. The house was one story, like hers, but it was gray and a lot longer. In the front yard were a tire swing, a red tricycle, a small orange slide, and a black-and-gray bicycle. It looked like the home of two boys, and Isla guessed she'd gotten the right house. She stealthily walked up to the house and onto the porch, carefully cupped her hands over the first window, and looked inside. This appeared to be the living room. There was an old piano, a little stone fireplace, and a long black couch. She slowly walked across the creaky porch to the next window. As she looked in, she smiled. This room looked like a boy's room. It appeared to be space themed, and up against the window was a bed with a boy in it. Isla looked at him for a minute, trying to make sure that it was Cash and not his little brother, but she decided the boy was too tall to be a preschooler. Taking a deep breath, Isla gently knocked on the window. At first, he didn't stir. So she knocked again.

The boy slowly looked up at Isla with blurry eyes. Then he shot up in bed, wide awake, looking as if he'd seen a ghost. Isla smiled and waved, hoping that he would recognize her. His scared face turned into a confused one. He crawled up to the window and carefully opened it.

"Isla? What are you doing here?" he whispered.

Isla smiled. "Wanna solve a mystery?"

"Isla, it's like, midnight!" Cash exclaimed as he glanced at his clock.

"So, are you coming or not?"

Cash snorted. "Of course I am," he said, as if there hadn't been any doubt. "But first let me get changed. I'll meet you by the road."

Isla leapt off the porch. Somehow, now she didn't feel like she needed to be so quiet. She sat in the tire swing and slowly swung back and forth, occasionally hitting mosquitoes. A few minutes later, Cash climbed out of the window with blue jeans, a black shirt, and a backpack. He carefully walked off the porch and made his way toward Isla.

"Good thinking, we might need that backpack," Isla whispered as they started down the road.

"So, what's going on exactly?" Cash asked.

"While I was at the hospital, my dad told me that the police suspected arson. I'm not supposed to be out here until they catch the bad guys! We need to go back to where the fire started and see if we can find anything that the police didn't find."

"Wait, you're saying someone set that fire on *purpose*?" Cash demanded.

"It also means we weren't alone that day," Isla said grimly.

"I bet they set that other fire too," Cash said, angry.

"But why would someone want to set fires on our land? What do they get out of it?" Isla wondered.

Cash gasped, "Isla! I've got it!"

"What!" Isla asked hopefully.

"Remember when we heard noise on the neighboring property? Maybe they accidentally burned your land while trying to clear theirs out."

Isla considered this. "I guess that makes sense."

They hopped over the gate and crawled through the barbed wire.

"Is there another gate? One they might have driven through by mistake?" Cash asked as they trudged through the brush.

"There might be an old one toward the back," Isla replied. She thought of something else then. "Hang on, what about the green Xes and the disc? Those were on our property, too. Could someone really make that many mistakes?"

Cash's face fell. "I guess not."

Isla stopped abruptly. Cash immediately stopped and listened, trying to figure out why she had halted. Isla pointed. Something was moving in the brush ahead. She slowly approached it. She looked down into the brush and saw two little brown eyes gazing up at her. Relieved, Isla smiled and motioned for Cash to come closer.

"What is it?" he whispered.

"It's a coyote pup," Isla replied.

Cash shined a flashlight on it, and they immediately saw what was wrong. The poor thing was stuck in a plant full of thorns. It yelped at the light and squirmed even harder.

"Shhhhh, it's OK," Isla soothed it.

She crouched down and started trying to get it free. Gently putting her hand under its stomach, she untangled him from the thorny branches. When he was finally free, Isla pressed his squirming body against her and brought him into the light.

"Is he hurt?" Cash asked worriedly.

"That's what I'm trying to find out," Isla said as she searched him for thorns and cuts. He was about six weeks old. His brown coat was covered in fleas.

"It looks like he just has a few scratches," Isla said as she tried to keep him still.

"Where do you think he lives?" Cash asked.

Isla shrugged and stood up. "There's a coyote den not too far from here. We can let him go close to there."

The pup whined and kicked, but Isla held him securely and tried to calm him down.

"Is this the first time you've held a coyote?" Cash asked as they walked.

"Yes. I usually don't try to touch them," Isla replied, "but there have been a couple times that I've helped them get out of sticky situations."

The pup looked up at Isla with eyes full of fear and confusion. He tried and tried to kick and snap his way out of her arms. Letting out a long sigh, he eventually gave up and lay limp in her arms. Isla could tell that he was malnourished and had been struggling in the bush for a while.

The den came into sight. Isla held out her arm and stopped Cash from going any further. She slowly crouched down and put the puppy on the ground. The puppy sped off toward the den, whining all the way for his mom.

"Let's go before we scare them," Isla whispered as she gestured to her left.

They walked away without speaking a word. Crickets and cicadas filled the air with noise. Cash jumped as a frog started croaking in front of them.

"Sure is scarier at night," Cash whispered as he walked closer to Isla. "How did you ever do this by yourself?"

Isla looked around. "I could then because animals don't scare me, but I don't think I could now," she admitted quietly, stepping a bit closer to her friend, glad he'd come with her. She bit her lip. She didn't like how things were changing.

"Don't worry. We'll figure out what's going on, and everything will be normal again," Cash promised her.

Isla looked at him. She hoped he was right.

"I had a pretty crazy day today," she told him, trying to change the subject.

"What happened?"

"This lady named Carroll took me shopping, and I freed a couple bunnies from their cage," Isla said with a mischievous grin.

"Seriously? I wish I was there!" Cash exclaimed.

"Me too," Isla laughed. "You would have loved it! It was just like one of your games. We ran over tables and through crowds until I opened the door and they were free!"

"Did you get in trouble?"

"Oh, yes," Isla said with a chuckle. "I've never seen my dad so flustered. We had to pay for the rabbits, and I'm pretty sure I'm grounded."

"Grounded? How long?" Cash asked.

Isla shook her head. "I don't know. I think my dad was too mad today to talk to me about it yet, and maybe he wanted to call my mom too."

"At least you got a good story out of it," Cash laughed as they stepped over a fallen tree.

"After that, I went to my dad's work and saw some of my new favorite people."

Cash elbowed her gently. "What about me?" He grinned.

Isla shoved him back playfully. "I said *some* of my favorite people. You're still my best friend," she promised him.

The words "best friend" echoed in her head. Even though he had been her best friend for over a month, sometimes the idea of finally having a best friend still felt strange and wonderful to her.

"Anyway, there's a couple whose names are Darrel and Carroll, and they're kinda like my grandparents. There's also this one man who I really like to talk to named Alexander. He's like my dad's brother, so he's basically my uncle. You should meet him someday, he's really awesome!"

A soft sound drifted through the air. The two froze and listened.

"It's that beeping again," Cash whispered.

"I wish we could go to the back of the property, but it would take too long," Isla whispered sadly.

"Maybe your dad will agree to drive us there."

"Maybe," Isla replied as she walked on. "So, my dad told me a little, but what happened after I left you two days ago?"

"Well, I started off walking along a game trail," Cash said. "At some point, something scared me—don't remember what—and I climbed a tree just like you said. After sitting there a minute, I started to smell smoke. Then I heard a scream. Before I knew it, I was running through the woods toward the smoke. Then I saw you lying on the ground." He paused and gulped. "Isla, I thought you were dead."

"Oh, I'm sorry for scaring you," she said.

"It's OK. Unless you did it on purpose," he teased.

Isla playfully hit his arm.

"Anyway, I ran over to you and soon saw the fire coming. Your head was bleeding, and you wouldn't wake up, so I carried you. At some point, you groaned, which actually made me feel better. You were so quiet and still. The fire was growing fast, but I made it to the barbed wire. I left you by the fence because I couldn't figure out how to take you with me. Then I heard fire trucks, and I ran to them to get you help."

It was almost exactly like her dad had told her, but hearing it again just made her realize her dad had been right: Cash had probably saved her life. "Wow," Isla said, almost in disbelief. "Thank you."

Cash blushed and waved a hand. "No problem."

They came upon a meadow. The moonlight shined on the tall, swaying grass and flowers. It looked both spooky and beautiful at the same time.

"You first," Cash said.

Isla stepped out of the shadows. Cash slowly followed behind. Isla could tell he was worried about someone or something seeing them in the clearing. She tried to be brave and reassure herself that the whole fire was just some sort of accident. It was bone-chillingly quiet, nothing but crickets and locusts.

"I don't like this," Cash said shakily.

"We're almost there," Isla encouraged him, but they both sighed a breath of relief as they stepped back into the shadows of the trees.

"We shouldn't be too far from the place where it started," Isla said.

Cash shook his head. "I don't recognize any of this. It all looks so different at night. What happens if we get lost?"

Isla shrugged. "We'll stay the night in a tree until morning."

"My mom's going to kill me," Cash groaned.

Isla thought that if her dad found out she'd gone exploring, he'd probably move them to a hotel far away. "There it is!" Isla exclaimed as the hill where she'd fallen came into view.

She ran ahead, hearing Cash's steps pounding heavy and loud behind her. She stopped at the top of the hill and looked down. She swallowed. Everything was black and lifeless. It still smelled strongly of fire.

Isla looked over at her friend and offered Cash her hand to keep them both from sliding down the hill again and for reassurance. He nodded, his face full of concern. They slowly made their way down the hill, occasionally slipping. Their little buddy system worked surprisingly well. Every time one of them slipped, the other managed to keep their balance.

"What do you think we'll find?" Cash asked as they neared the bottom.

"I don't know. Just look for anything that don't seem right," Isla replied.

They reached the bottom, and Isla let go of Cash's sweaty hand. The wind whistled through the surrounding trees, giving the area an even eerier feel.

"We should take turns standing guard," Cash suggested.

It was a good idea. Isla nodded. Cash gulped and looked through the trees. Isla slowly walked around, scanning for something out of the ordinary. She tried to remember what she had seen before she fell. *A snake. I was too busy looking at that snake.* She ventured into the trees. It was harder to see in their shadows, but not quite impossible. She walked and walked until Cash was almost out of sight.

"Oh, no," Isla mumbled.

Cash heard her. "What!"

"Tire tracks," Isla called.

Cash ran over to her. By the looks of it, the vehicle had come from deeper in the forest, stopped, then turned back around.

"Maybe they're from the firemen," Cash suggested.

Isla shook her head. Her dad had told her more about the fire when they'd gotten home from the hospital. "They couldn't get the trucks in, so they used helicopters."

"Wait, helicopters? Why didn't you tell me?"

"I was too focused on how it started, not how it was put out."

"But *helicopters*? How could you leave that awesome detail out!" Cash looked at Isla, shocked.

Isla just shrugged. "Let's focus on the mysterious tracks. Maybe it was arson after all."

Cash was worried. He looked around. "You think they're still around?"

"I sure hope not." Isla tried to see where the tracks led. "Let's follow 'em," she decided.

"Follow them?" Cash exclaimed in a whisper. "You're joking, right?"

"How else are we going to solve anything?" Isla asked.

He stared at her for a second, looking torn. "I want to. This is so cool, but, Isla, you almost died just two days ago." He looked up at her bandaged head and winced.

Isla looked into his eyes. "I'm scared too," she told him. "But we have to solve this before it gets worse."

He thought for a moment. "OK, let's do it."

Isla led the way. They both walked slowly and quietly, both ready to bolt just in case something were to happen. The tracks winded through the woods. They had obviously been made by a large vehicle, for its tires had crushed and flattened everything in their path.

"It must have taken them a long time to drive through this," Isla whispered.

"Do you think they were trying to kill you or that they didn't know you were there?" Cash asked.

Isla shivered. "I hope they weren't trying to kill me. And if they were, how did they know where I was?"

Cash paused and looked at her. Both of them opened their eyes wide as they came to the same conclusion. "You don't think they're watching us, do you?" Cash whispered.

They both looked all around.

Isla bit her lip. "I've never seen any cameras," she said. "If they were trying to get me, they probably just happened to see me," she said. She didn't know whom she was trying to convince more—Cash or herself.

"I hope so," he said shakily.

They carefully continued on. Owls hooted around them, frogs croaked in the distance, and trees scraped against each other. Despite the heat, both Isla and Cash had chills and goose bumps. Suddenly, the tires ended up ahead.

"What?" Isla said, confused.

Cash looked all around. "They can't just stop!"

"Where's your flashlight?" Isla whispered.

Cash quickly pulled it out and shined it ahead of them. They gasped and slowly looked up at what looked like a large, camouflaged net. They both stood there, breathing heavily, as Cash shined his flashlight all around it. The net covered something that was far taller than them and at least ten feet wide.

"Um," Isla gulped. "You wanna pull the net up and look while I watch?"

"Why can't I stand watch?" Cash asked.

"Because it's my turn," she said. "I'll be right here, and I'll follow when you say the coast is clear."

"But what if it isn't clear?"

"Then we run for it."

Cash slowly lifted the bottom of the net with his free hand while shining the flashlight on it with his other hand.

"Whoa," he muttered.

"What, what is it!" Isla asked.

Cash shined his flashlight all around. "I think the coast is clear. You *gotta* see this."

They walked under the net and let it drop behind them. Isla gasped; the net was hiding the entrance to a cave. Cash shined the flashlight onto a big red truck in the middle of the entrance. It was scraped up, had dents all over, was missing the door to its bed, and had huge tires. Clearly the truck that had made the tracks. They made their way around it. Cash reached up to grab the front door handle and slowly hoisted himself up to see if anyone was inside.

He sighed a breath of relief. "No one's inside."

Isla helped him down. She could feel her heart beating at an alarming rate. She wondered if he were just as scared as her. Cash shined his flashlight around. A little deeper into the cave, there was a pile of tires and gasoline.

"These tires are a lot smaller," Cash whispered as they approached them. "And they're flat."

Isla turned one over to reveal part of a mesquite tree jutting out of it. "I bet they thought these tires would work out here."

Cash lifted a gas can with ease. "These are empty. Do you think they used these to start the fire?"

Isla shook her head. "My dad said they used ker-, kero-, um, kero-somethin' to start the fire," she said.

Cash shined his flashlight deeper into the cave. "How far do you think it goes?"

"I don't know. I've never seen this cave before," Isla said.

They walked further in. The cave started to slope downward, but it only took them a few seconds to find the end. The ceiling came down just above their heads. Isla gasped and pulled Cash backwards just before his head hit a bat.

Cash stumbled back and exclaimed, "What? What's wrong?"

She pointed up at the little brown bat. "I was wondering where the bats were coming from. I'd seen them at night in the past but never found a cave."

She watched as Cash shined his flashlight around it.

"See, there's bat poop all over the ceiling." She looked down. "And you're stepping in some."

Cash jumped back. "Where!"

Isla giggled. "I'm just kidding, but there is some in front of us." She pointed.

"That's a lot for one bat," Cash said.

"Oh, I'm sure there's a bunch more. They're nocturnal and won't be back till later. I learned about them in science."

"Will they attack us?" Cash asked worriedly.

"I don't *think* so, but I've never really been around them before."

"Let's hurry up just in case they or someone else comes back," Cash said.

Isla nodded. Cash shined the light all around, but there was nothing else around them. They made their way back up to the entrance.

"Isla, are you going to tell your dad about the cave?" Cash whispered.

She bit her lip. "He sure won't be happy when he hears what we've done."

"What if you just told him that you'd found a cave before that would be a perfect hiding place for someone?" Cash asked.

Isla brightened. "I could do that. I'll tell him first thing in the morning." She glanced around the cave. "You see anything else?"

Cash looked one more time. "I don't see nothin'," he said. "Can we start heading back? This place is giving me the heebie-jeebies."

"Yeah, I don't want to be here any longer than we have to," Isla agreed, but as she headed toward the net, she noticed something in the dirt.

"Wait, Cash, shine your light over there," Isla said as she pointed toward the edge of the cave.

She quickly ran over to the edge, trying to stay out of the light so she wouldn't block it from shining onto the ground. She pulled a small, worn piece of paper out of the dirt.

"What is it?" Cash asked anxiously.

Isla held the paper into the light. It was tattered and torn, but one word could be made out.

"Cagney," Isla muttered. "Does that mean anything to you?"

"No, I've never heard that before," Cash said.

"Hmm, we'd better hang onto this," Isla said as she carefully stuck it in her pocket.

They headed back toward the camouflaged net. Isla lifted it and let Cash go under first.

"You can put the flashlight up. It'll be harder for anything to see us without it," Isla whispered.

Cash quickly put it up and stepped closer toward Isla. They walked shoulder to shoulder, both even more scared than before now that they knew for sure that someone had been on the property. Isla looked all around, expecting to see a face in the woods at any moment. She wanted to close her eyes, but she had to concentrate. One wrong turn and they'd be outside all night trying to get home. She tried not to think about that;

she was already scared enough. Something rustled in the brush ahead of them. They both froze.

"Isla?" Cash squeaked.

"Shhh," Isla hushed.

She concentrated hard on the brush, straining her eyes to see what was inside. She tried to slow her breathing so she could hear better, but both she and Cash were panting like dogs. Her imagination was racing, making the little rustle seem like far more. Suddenly, a raccoon sprang forth from the brush. Cash and Isla jumped back and ran, screaming. The raccoon chased them for a moment, then stopped. Feeling foolish, Isla stopped herself and grabbed Cash before he could get any further. The raccoon stared at them, seemed to be pleased with himself, and then went back into the brush.

"What was that?" Cash exclaimed as he tried to catch his breath.

Isla burst out laughing. "A raccoon. It was just a raccoon."

"I don't think it's funny. It tried to kill us!" Cash cried.

Isla put her hand on his shoulder to steady herself as she laughed, "I can't help it. I think the stress is getting to me. It wasn't trying to kill us, just get rid of us."

"Well, it did a swell job," Cash huffed.

"C'mon, let's just get home."

CHAPTER THIRTEEN

"Rise and shine!" Isla's dad shouted.

Isla groggily opened her eyes and groaned.

"What time is it?" she asked with a yawn.

"Seven o'clock. We gotta get! You're coming with me to work, remember?" he exclaimed as he started looking through Isla's new clothes.

Isla groaned, rubbing her burning eyes. She and Cash hadn't gotten home until 5:30 a.m. Isla tried to do the math in her head. *One hour of sleep? Maybe thirty minutes?* She could never figure out any math problems when she was half asleep.

"Go ahead and wash your stitches before you get changed," her dad said.

He flung jeans and a horse shirt on the bed. The shirt was all white except for a red-and-white paint horse on the front. The horse looked like a beautiful painting. Isla looked at the clothes, confused.

"Did you just pick out my clothes for me?"

"That one's my favorite," he said with smile. "Now get up, and get ready!"

She slowly swung her legs out of bed. Her dad walked out of the room, and she slowly followed. She made her way to the bathroom. She had never felt so groggy. She half expected to run into a wall at any moment. She turned on the bathroom light and squinted in the mirror. Her dirty blonde hair looked more like a rat's nest. She sniffed her arm. It smelled of sweat and dirt. Usually she wouldn't care. But she was going to see more people today, and maybe a bath would help her wake up.

"Hey, Dad? I think I'm just gonna take a shower," she shouted.

Her dad suddenly appeared around the corner.

"Are you feeling OK?"

"Just . . . peachy!" she yawned.

"I don't think I've ever heard you say you wanted a shower," he said with a smile.

Isla stretched and shrugged. "It'll probably be the last time."

Isla stared out the truck window. She couldn't believe they were leaving the property *again*. She felt as if she were missing out on so much. The deer might have even forgotten her by now, and what if something happened to Sammy, Piper, or Acorn? They had to catch the arsonists so her parents would let her back out there for real.

Remembering Cash's suggestion, she turned to her dad. "Hey, Dad?"

"Yeah?"

"I think you should tell the police that there's a cave near the area where the fire was set. If anyone wanted to hide anything, it would be in there," she explained.

"OK, thanks for telling me. I'll call them when we get to the office." He paused and looked at her thoughtfully. "Since when do we have a cave?"

"I have no idea. Cash and I found it very recently," Isla admitted.

"That reminds me. I have a surprise for you," her dad said as he stopped the truck.

He jumped out to open the gate. Isla was tempted to honk the horn but instead rolled down her window.

"What sort of surprise?"

"You'll see!" he shouted as he opened the gate.

Isla slumped back into the seat. Hadn't there been enough surprises already? Her dad hopped back in and started down the road.

"I thought you turned left to get to work," she said confusedly.

"We gotta pick up something first."

Isla's face lit up. "Cash?"

Her dad smiled. Isla sat up straighter, suddenly wide awake.

"I called his mom this morning and asked if he'd like to tag along. He said yes."

"I'll hop in the back so he's not alone!" Isla unbuckled and climbed over the seat.

Her dad laughed. "Next time wait till we stop?" he suggested.

"OK!" Isla shouted as she fell off of the headrest and onto the back seat.

She buckled up just as they turned into Cash's little dirt driveway. Cash was waiting on the porch. He looked as if he were half asleep. He was wearing jeans and a gray shirt that appeared to be on backwards. Isla reached over and opened his door so he'd know which side was his. He ran to the car and climbed in.

"Hi, Cash, how are you?" Christopher asked with a smile.

"I'm good, sir. Thank you for inviting me," Cash replied shyly.

"You're welcome. I figured y'all would want to hang out," Christopher said.

Isla leaned over and whispered into Cash's ear, "Your shirt's on backwards."

Cash looked down. "Whoops," he muttered.

He pulled his arms inside his shirt and turned it around. It had a picture of a wolf on it.

"What are *we* gonna do at the office while you work?" Isla asked her dad.

"I'm sure y'all will find something."

"I've never seen so many boxes!" Cash shouted as they explored the office.

They had found a huge storage room full of stuff. He picked up an old phone that was bigger than his head. "You think it'll work? It's missing its screen."

Isla looked at it and laughed, "Those don't got screens."

Cash looked at her, confused. "How are you s'posed to know who's calling?"

"You answer it."

"I think I'd prefer a smartphone." Cash laid down the phone and opened a box. "Packing peanuts? I've never seen these before in real life!"

He dug his hands into the box and grabbed handfuls of them.

"I ate one once. It was like a flavorless Cheeto," Isla said as she fiddled with a computer mouse.

"What's that?" Cash asked. He ran to a door that was cracked open. Isla dropped the mouse and followed. There was no light coming through the door. Isla slowly opened it. It was a small, old, abandoned office.

"Whoa," they both said in unison. There was a dusty brown shelf half full of books, an old brown desk covered with random things, a tall lamp, a gray spinning chair, and a few boxes. Cash flipped a switch on the lamp. It flickered before turning on.

"Did someone get fired . . . or *die*?" Cash asked.

"I'm not sure; it looks like no one's been in here for decades."

Isla slowly sat on the chair. It creaked like no other. They started looking through the desk. It had all kinds of keys, paperclips, pens, papers, key rings, and things on it.

"This pen's from Tennessee," Cash said as he picked up a blue pen.

"The date on this paper says February 10, 1993!" Isla exclaimed.

"This is so cool. I bet these keys open all kinds of secret things," Cash said as he picked a few up. "This one says 'house' on it!"

Isla picked up another. "This one says 'safe' on it." She looked at Cash. "You'd think they'd protect these."

"Unless they're dead," Cash reminded her.

"If they had died, someone would have collected their things. These were left on purpose." She opened a drawer and found a dusty picture frame. "This must be them!"

The picture showed a tall, half-bald man with his wife. He was wearing a tuxedo, and he had black hair that was combed over to help conceal his baldness. His wife had long, red hair, a red dress, and pearls around her neck. It looked like they were at a party.

"This looks old. He probably retired," Isla said.

Cash picked up a sticky note that was under the picture frame.

"Look, here's a note with just the number 928 written on it. Another mystery. I feel like we're detectives!" Cash said excitedly. A voice called their names in the distance.

"That's probably my dad," Isla sighed. They jumped up and ran to his office.

"What have y'all been up to?" Christopher asked them. He was signing papers at his desk. His glasses looked as if they were about to fall off his nose. Isla reached forward and pushed them back.

"Exploring. What happened to that old, empty office?" Isla asked.

"Old, empty office . . ." he muttered as he tapped his pen on the desk. "You mean the one in the storage room?"

"Yeah, that one," she nodded.

"I believe that belonged to an employee we had a while back. His name was . . . Cagney, Bill Cagney."

Isla gasped so violently she had a coughing fit.

"Are you OK?" Her dad asked, startled.

"Yeah, I'm fine," Isla said, trying to hide her excitement.

"Is he dead?" Cash asked with wide eyes.

"No, he retired a long time ago. As far as I know he's still around."

"He left his home key," Isla said.

"Yeah, I think he left everything. I forget just why. We just kept it all back there in his office." Her dad shook his head. "Anyway, I called y'all because Alexander just got here and he wants to see you. His office is a few doors to the left."

Isla burst out in a smile. She grabbed Cash's arm and headed down the hall. They found Alexander's door and peeked around the corner. He was typing out an email. Isla gently knocked.

"Hey, squirt!" he exclaimed as he took off his glasses.

"Hi! This is Cash," she said as they walked up to his desk.

"So, you're the hero I've heard about," Alexander said.

He reached his arm out and shook Cash's hand. Cash blushed shyly and rubbed the back of his neck.

"Yep, he saved me from that fire," Isla said proudly.

"It's a good thing y'all have each other," Alexander said. "What started the fire, anyway?"

"The firefighters think it's arson," Isla said.

"Arson? Who would want to do arson out there in the sticks? It wouldn't really affect much," Alexander said thoughtfully.

Isla and Cash glanced at each other. "We think the property might be being developed," she said.

"But there's nothing around y'all's place for at least an hour."

"I found a CD with plans for some sort of park."

Alexander shrugged. "Hmm. Maybe someone's trying to buy land up there to build one."

"I sure hope not! I don't want them scaring all the animals off."

"Me, neither," said Cash.

"That wouldn't be good." Alexander looked at the clock. "I don't have much work today. Y'all want to go do something?"

CHAPTER FOURTEEN

"Where to first?" Alexander asked as they drove down the road in his huge white truck.

Isla shifted in her seat excitedly and looked out the window. "What's around these parts?" she asked.

"Well, we have this milkshake place, a little Mexican food joint, a shooting range, a pottery barn, and an antique store. Anything else would be in the next town."

Cash's face lit up. "Could we please get milkshakes?"

Alexander laughed, "I don't see why not."

Cash and Isla bounced up and down. Isla hadn't had a milkshake in years. Alexander pulled into the drive-through. "What flavor?" he asked, rubbing his chin.

"Oreo, please!" Cash cried.

"Me too," Isla said after reading the menu. She hadn't realized so many flavors existed. Alexander ordered two small Oreo milkshakes and a brownie milkshake. They said their thank yous as they headed back down the road.

"Now what?" Alexander asked.

"Could we go to that antique store?" Isla asked with a mouth full of Oreo goodness.

"Sure," Alexander said.

He made a sharp turn onto a smaller road. Old buildings slowly started appearing along the road as he drove.

Alexander cleared his throat. "You said y'all found a CD. Did you find anything else?"

Isla looked at Cash, wondering what all they should tell.

"We haven't found much," Cash said, looking at Isla.

Isla nodded, grateful. He was right. Alexander was her dad's best friend. They didn't want him knowing how much they'd been looking out on the property. "Yeah, just the CD," Isla said.

"Sounds like things are getting pretty dangerous on the property," Alexander said. "Isla, are you and your dad staying on the property, or are y'all staying somewhere else until things calm down?"

"Staying on the property," Isla replied.

"I hope y'all aren't still exploring. I'd hate for one of y'all to get hurt again," Alexander said. He sounded concerned.

"We'll be fine," Isla assured him. "As long as Cash and I stick together and stay on our guard, I don't think anything else will happen."

Alexander looked at her through the rearview mirror and smiled. "I hope so, squirt, but y'all better be real careful. These people sound dangerous."

"We'll be careful," Isla said.

Alexander turned into an old parking lot. The concrete was covered with cracks and old gum. The antique store looked more like a white barn. The door was old and had a string of bells on its handle. They all hopped out and walked toward the entrance.

"Y'all need to finish your shakes first. They don't want us ruining anything," Alexander said as he threw his cup into a green trash can.

Isla and Cash scarfed down the last of their shakes and threw their cups away.

Inside, the shop smelled very strange, and the air seemed thicker. It had blue carpet, a wood desk in the front, and rows of random things. Behind the desk was an elderly woman wearing a floral dress. Her head was covered in thin white curls that went to her shoulders. Her glasses had beaded string attached to the sides that connected behind her head.

"How may I help you?" she asked with a warm smile.

"We're just looking," Alexander said kindly as they began to explore. "Don't break more than you can buy," he warned before going his own way.

Cash and Isla slowly walked down the first aisle. "Look at this!" Cash exclaimed as he picked up a vintage camera.

Isla admired it, thinking how her mom would love it, but told him, "Careful, it looks fragile."

She picked up an old toy across the aisle. It was a stuffed brown bear with a plastic orange face. The face was covered with makeup, and one eye was half closed.

"I do not understand this," she said.

Cash made a face. "That's creepy! Put it down before it possesses you."

Isla carefully put the scary bear back on the shelf, demented face toward the wall. The next section was full of old CDs and books. Cash and Isla walked through them until they reached the end, a section full of random old items.

"This wolf statue looks just like your shirt," Isla said, picking up a small wolf.

Cash was interested. "How much is it?" he asked.

Isla checked the price tag on the bottom. "It's *fifty* dollars!" she gasped.

"You'd better put that back gently!" Cash advised, backing away.

Isla gently put the wolf back. They both started sifting through a pile of posters that lay next to the statue.

"Hey, Cash?" Isla whispered.

"What?"

Isla looked all around to make sure no one was near, then walked forward so they were more concealed by the dividing walls.

"Remember that piece of paper we found?" she asked.

"Yeah?"

"It said 'Cagney,'" Isla whispered.

Cash's face lit up. "Like in the office? You know, I was wondering why Bill Cagney sounded so familiar."

"Do you think he has anything to do with this?" Isla asked.

"Probably. Why else would his name be in that cave?"

Isla nodded. "We should probably explore around the cave some more."

"Hey kids, come look at this!" Alexander shouted from across the store, interrupting the two's conversation.

They walked back through the store, glancing at every aisle as they went. They soon found Alexander admiring a colorful jukebox.

"Have you ever seen one of these?" he asked.

Cash nodded. "I saw one on TV once."

Isla shook her head. "What is it?"

"A jukebox," Alexander explained. "An old music player. They used to have them in restaurants and dance halls. You'd put a nickel in it, and then you would choose a song for it to play," Alexander said as he pointed to the different parts. "See the old records?"

Isla stood on her tiptoes and tried to get a good look. Alexander picked her up.

"Wow, there's a bunch of them," Isla exclaimed. "Do you think it still works?"

Alexander set her down. "I doubt it."

He started pushing buttons, and Cash joined him.

"I'd buy it, but it's very expensive," Alexander said.

"I'd buy it, if I had any money," Cash muttered as he pressed every single button. "Kids my age can't even get a job."

"We should get going. Your dad wanted y'all back before lunch," Alexander said, looking at his watch. He grinned guilt-ily. "Oh, and please don't tell him I loaded y'all with sugar."

Isla and Cash promised faithfully to keep that their little secret.

"So what did y'all do?" Isla's dad asked as Isla and Cash sat down in his office.

"We went to an antique store and saw a bunch of cool stuff," Isla said.

"I wish I was rich. Then I could buy some of that awesome junk," Cash sighed.

Her dad laughed, "I think you'd buy other things, like monster trucks, go-karts, and mansions."

"Those too," Cash said.

"When are we going back home?" Isla asked.

"We'll leave in a couple of hours. Y'all can go explore some more until then. There's some food in the break room if you two get hungry," her dad said before digging through a large stack of paper.

Cash jumped up and headed toward the break room right away. Isla quickly followed. The word 'explore' gave her a bad feeling in the pit of her stomach. For a few minutes, she had actually forgotten about the fires and why she had to go to her dad's work in the first place.

"I feel like I haven't eaten in days!" Cash announced as they walked into the break room.

"We literally *just* ate about thirty minutes ago," Isla said.

She watched Cash raid the fridge. "Yeah, but it really wasn't much," Cash said. He pulled out a bag of leftover pepperoni pizza. "How about this?"

Isla shrugged. "I guess so."

Cash placed the top of the bag in his mouth and started to search the cabinets. He pulled out two paper plates, opened the bag, and put the pizza on them.

"How can you eat when so much is going on?" Isla asked him as he put the pizza in the microwave.

"What do you mean?" Cash asked.

"We need to figure out this whole arson thing. I want things to go back to normal already."

Cash looked over his shoulder at Isla. "Maybe this is a job for the professionals," he said sadly. "We're just kids."

"But we have to protect our land."

Cash wasn't so sure. "I don't know. Last night was pretty scary."

"I can't do this without you, Cash," Isla pleaded.

Cash shifted and thrust his hands in his pockets. "I don't want you to get hurt again," he explained. "You didn't see that fire, Isla. I did. We could die out there."

Isla's lip quivered. "Are you giving up?"

Cash took the pizza out and laid it down on the table. "I don't know," he muttered. They sat down and stared at the pizza.

"You seemed so ready to solve this mystery last night," Isla eventually said.

"I was. But it was better when I thought it was an accident. Someone's really out there. Honestly, last night freaked me out."

"We could try do go during the daytime," Isla suggested.

"Maybe," Cash said noncommittally. He slowly picked up a slice and started to eat. Isla stared into space and thought about the whole situation. Maybe if they hid in a tree near the back gate, they could take a picture of anyone who trespassed. But if Cash refused to come, she would be all alone if something went wrong. He had a point—they were just kids. But she just couldn't convince herself to give up. She was way too protective of the beautiful land she called home. She set her teeth and clenched her fists, suddenly angry and determined to stop all of this.

"Are you OK? You look tense." Cash said.

"I'm fine," Isla snapped.

Cash hesitated, looking over at her guiltily. "Are you mad at me?" he asked.

"No, not you."

"Then what are you mad at?"

"I'm mad at whoever is messing with our land. They will regret this."

Her angry tone seemed to scare him. "Are you going to kill them?" Cash asked. His voice quivered.

Isla looked at him, exasperated. "Of course not! Why do you always end up talking about killing people and dying? I'll just call the police and hope they go to jail for a very long time."

"Oh, good!" Cash said, relieved. "But seriously, please try to stay away from trouble."

Isla nodded and picked up a slice. Cash seemed happy that she was finally eating.

"I thought I heard a familiar voice!" a voice suddenly called out.

Cash and Isla almost jumped right out of their skin. Isla shot her head back to see Darrel in the doorway.

"Hi, Darrel!" Isla chirped, jumping up to hug him.

"Who's this handsome young man?" Darrel asked.

Cash blushed. "I'm Cash."

"He's the one who saved me," Isla said.

Darrel crossed his arms, playing tough. "And are y'all dating, or just friends?"

"Friends," they both quickly said.

Darrel laughed, "That's what they all say at first."

Cash huffed, annoyed. "I don't know why I can't be friends with a girl without everyone saying I like her all of a sudden," he complained. "All the kids at school are just the same. I can't hang out with some of the coolest people in the class without everyone talking!" He glanced worriedly at Isla. "Don't worry, you're cooler than everybody else," he assured her.

Isla smiled, pleased, and Darrel walked over to the coffee maker and started it. He patted Cash on the shoulder. "Don't worry, I'm just teasing you. I think it's great you two are friends," he said.

Isla sat back down and continued eating.

"So, have y'all figured out any more about this whole fire situation?" Darrel asked Isla.

Isla clenched her fist again. "Not yet," she said.

"Keep me updated. I'll be praying for y'all," Darrel said as he left the room with his coffee. Isla watched him leave.

"So, would you really not join me if I did some more exploring?" Isla asked while Cash stuffed his mouth.

Cash swallowed. "I don't know. Ask me after I've gotten more sleep."

CHAPTER FIFTEEN

Isla couldn't wait for Cash to get more sleep. She paced her bedroom floor, her determination to fix all this blazing inside her like the fires the arsonists had started. It was only 5:00 p.m., and she just had to do something. Cash was too exhausted to come with her. He was back home by now, and even her dad had gone to bed early, but Isla didn't understand how anyone could sleep at a time like this. The arsonists could be trespassing right now, but no one would know because everyone was asleep.

"Ugh!" she shouted.

She looked at all the pictures on her wall. At the end of the timeline that had been all animals and happiness were a bunch of pictures of burnt-up land and sadness. Isla was getting more and more desperate.

"Someone needs to do something," she whispered. She took a deep breath. Her brown Texas shirt and ripped jeans were lying on the bed, practically begging to be worn again. She slowly put them on.

"*I* have to do something," she told herself as she grabbed her mom's camera bag. For a moment, she stood there quietly.

Then, she was ready.

Usually she ran to the barbed-wire fence gleefully, antic-ipating the day ahead. Now she practically marched. Sammy ran up a tree and watched her with those beady eyes, but she barely even noticed him. The brush had never really bothered her too much before, but now all she wanted was a machete. Stickers started to tangle her long hair. She knew it would only get worse. It would take all night to reach the back gate—not all the way at the back of their ten thousand acres, but still very, very far. A wasp buzzed in front of her face. She didn't care. She had a mission. She was determined.

The sun was low in the sky. Coyotes started to howl. They'd be hunting right about now. Isla imagined what Cash would say if he were there. He'd probably start to freak out if he heard the coyotes. She wished he were there all the same. She'd feel so much safer with him around, but she couldn't wait.

Alexander's words echoed in her head. *"It's a good thing y'all have each other."*

Why had he hesitated, anyway, Isla wondered. Suddenly she *was* mad at him, and she scoffed. She remembered what she'd told him, that she didn't think she could go out here on her own now. He probably thought his absence would keep her from investigating. But she'd been silly. She hadn't ever needed a friend before she met him, and she didn't need a friend now.

It was getting late, but the sun still seemed to beat down. It already felt like a sauna. She wiped the sweat from her forehead and neck. Birds of all kinds were singing every-where. Usually she would join in, but there was no time for that now. Her constant stomping through the brush almost drowned out their calls.

But she still heard a soft whine from the grass. Isla stopped dead in her tracks. She looked all around. A few feet ahead of her was a coyote pup. Isla noticed the tears in its coat and its brown eyes. Could it be the same one she and Cash had rescued the night before? It reached its nose out, peering at Isla, and sniffed the air. Then it let out another whine.

"Go on," Isla told it. "Go back home."

It sat down and let out a pitiful howl. Isla sighed, exasperated.

"What are you doing here? Why are you out looking for trouble?" she demanded.

The pup cocked its head to the side and stared hard at her. "What are *you* doing looking for trouble?" it seemed to be asking. Isla stared back at it a second, shook her head, and continued. It stood up and whined again, refusing to move out of the path.

She stepped right over him. Trying not to look back was hard. She could practically feel his sad eyes on her. But he didn't follow or whine again.

"That was bizarre," she muttered, stepping over a fallen tree. Surely he hadn't learned to trust humans after that one night. The trees started to cast long shadows. She couldn't see the sun, but she knew from those shadows it had to be very low. It would be dark in about an hour.

Isla yawned. It was a few hours into the night. Unlike the night before, it was very dark and hard to navigate. The crickets were constantly chirping, and cicadas were incessantly buzzing. She almost couldn't hear her own steps. The wind rustled the trees all around. She came upon something large and white. Straining her eyes, she realized it was the skull and bones of a large cow.

"Where did that come from?" she asked aloud. They had never owned cattle in the past.

Her eyes widened. "The gate."

It had to be near. At some point someone must have opened it and accidentally let in a cow from the neighboring property. Her stomach started to turn. She wouldn't be prepared if the arsonist came and something went wrong. She quickly took a photo of the cow skull for evidence and moved on.

The gate was soon visible in the distance. Her steps slowed as she neared it. The brush stopped, and a large, dirt road was revealed. It was covered in tire tracks. The old gray gate was shut, but the lock and chains had been cut. Beyond the gate was a property much like theirs, except there were small rocks on its dirt road. It stretched out farther than the eye could see. Isla gulped as she picked up the old chains. They hadn't been cut the last time she had explored this area. She took another photo of the cut chains. Even if she didn't catch the arsonist tonight, she could take this evidence to the police, and they'd have a lead to follow. Scratching a mosquito bite, she pondered.

All of the surrounding trees were large oaks. If she climbed one, no one would be able to see her. She made sure the camera bag was secure around her neck and under her shoulder and made her way to a tree a little ways from the road. It was rather large and covered with green leaves. Isla noticed a bull snake resting toward the top. She picked up a long, thin stick and held it in her mouth as she climbed.

Once high enough, she secured herself on a branch below the snake. Ever so slowly, she managed to push the stick underneath the snake. Then, she flung it onto the next tree.

"I'm sorry, but I refuse to risk getting bit after coming this far," she shouted as it slithered across the other tree, looking annoyed its rest had been disturbed. Climbing a bit higher, she found a bigger branch to sit on. Bugs scattered in every direction. Her legs and arms were already covered in bites. Not scratching them was proving to be very difficult. She already had quite a few from the night before.

A faint shuffling and snorting sound could be heard beneath her. An armadillo was digging for grubs. They reminded Isla of tiny pigs when they did that. It snorted as it dug little holes here and there.

She sat in the tree, watching it root around for a while, hearing nothing but the sounds of the forest all around. An owl, the buzzing of the bugs. All of it made her sleepy. She'd been going on anger and an hour of sleep, but now that she'd stopped moving, her eyes were getting heavier and heavier.

"I'll just rest my eyes," she mumbled.

CHAPTER SIXTEEN

Suddenly awakened by a change in the noises around her, Isla's eyes fluttered open. The sun was shining on her face. She slowly sat up and looked around. The sun had just begun to rise. The birds—there were too few of them singing. Far fewer than was usual this time of day. Their silence had awakened her. Isla was almost too scared to look down at the gate, but she wiped her sweaty hands on her jeans and made herself look down. There was no one there, but she could hear a faint noise coming from the neighboring property, growing louder all the time. She slowly took out her camera and waited. Her little heart was racing, and her stomach was in a knot. Suddenly, she saw something.

A black truck was coming down the road in the distance. Dirt was flying behind it. The trespassers! Isla immediately regretted coming. Cash had been right: this was too dangerous. What if they saw her? What would they do?

With shaking hands, Isla took a picture of the truck as it neared the broken gate. The bed of the truck was concealed with a cover. Old mud and dents covered its sides. The truck stopped at the gate. Isla removed the previous photo and stuck it in her pocket, preparing to take another. A man with black hair stepped out on the driver's side. His skin was tan from the blazing sun. He wore an old gray shirt, brown boots, and torn jeans. He opened the gate. Isla snapped the picture. She pressed the camera against her shirt, trying to conceal the sound of it printing the picture.

She was so nervous, her stomach started to grumble loudly, but holding her stomach didn't seem to help. Sweat started to drip from her forehead. The man froze and looked around. Isla accidentally let out a little whimper. The man slowly got back into his truck and drove onto the property. But he didn't get out. Instead, he reached into his pocket and pulled something out.

"Please don't be a weapon, please don't be a weapon," Isla repeated under her breath.

He held the object up to his head and started moving his mouth. She was relieved to see this but developed a new fear. What if he had heard her and was calling a partner?

Isla swallowed. "There's two of them," she realized with a sickening, growing dread.

Isla felt as if she were going to throw up. It had been a good thirty minutes, and the man hadn't even budged. If only she had a gun or a phone. All she had was a camera. She had considered climbing down and running, but he could have a gun or maybe a Taser. Isla thought for the tenth time in the last half hour that her dad didn't even know where she was. She tried to calculate the distance she was from the truck. If he tried to get her, there could be enough time to climb down and start running before he reached the tree. She wished the bull snake would come back. Then she could throw it on him.

Isla's heart skipped a beat as a white truck came driving up the road, speeding over toward the gate. The man in the black truck stepped out and waited. The white truck stopped just before hitting the other truck. Isla leaned forward in an effort to get a better look. The black-haired man walked over to the white truck's door just as it started to open.

"Yes, I'm sure I heard someone," he said to the man. "It was probably that kid who lives here."

A man with a green Western shirt, jeans, and Western boots slowly got out of the white truck and shut the door. Isla strained her eyes to see him better, only to see a familiar face.

Her stomach dropped. Her mouth dropped open in shock. "Alexander?" she cried aloud, too surprised to remember to be quiet.

Both of the men quickly looked up at the tree. On instinct, Isla slid down the tree, scraping her shins on its trunk. Ignoring the sting of pain, she started running. All the animals had fled. She could hear nothing but the sound of her own heart pounding in her ears—and the stomping feet behind her.

"Isla! It's me!" Alexander shouted. "Stop, and we'll talk about this!"

Tears began to blur her vision. "We trusted you! Why are you doing this?" she shouted over her shoulder. Alexander, the trespasser? The arsonist? Her friend, her father's friend?

"This will all make sense if you just stop!" he shouted between ragged breaths.

But Isla wasn't about to stop. Something in her told her not to stop, no matter how much she wanted to believe him. A hundred thoughts raced through her mind. She could barely process any of them. This was a nightmare—just a crazy bad dream. Any moment now, her dad would wake her up, and everything would be back to normal.

But she didn't wake up. "Cash!" she cried. But it was hopeless. He probably wasn't even out here. He was probably still at home asleep. Isla looked around wildly for anything that might help. A rock, a snake, a hill Alexander wouldn't know and couldn't climb. His footsteps were louder behind her. Isla's feet tore across the rough, wild ground. She hissed as a sharp pain in her foot jolted her, but there was no time to see what was wrong, no time to watch her step or pick a better path.

"Isla!" Alexander yelled desperately.

Panicked, aware of everything around her, Isla was starting to recognize the area. This was where Piper lived. Which meant a certain ally of hers wasn't too far, she realized. She had a weapon.

"Ruckus," she gasped.

He wouldn't bite her, but he might bite one of them. She made a sharp turn and jumped into a clearing. Her eyes darted back and forth, searching for that dead tree.

"Isla...you can't...run forever," Alexander said breathlessly.

Isla's heart gave a leap; she could see the dead tree now.

"Please be home," she thought repeatedly as she tore through the grass toward it.

She bounded over the tree and continued straight on. Ruckus started to rattle, annoyed by these intruders.

"Argh!" the man with black hair screamed in pain.

Isla glanced back just in time to see the fallen man grab Alexander's ankle desperately.

"Don't leave me here!" he pleaded.

"Carlos! Let go!" Alexander yelled furiously.

"Thanks, Ruckus!" Isla shouted with a smile.

She came upon a large meadow, and her heart sank. If an area of brush and trees had appeared, there would have been time to hide. But the grass and wildflowers had grown past her shoulders now, so, having another thought, Isla ran toward the middle and lay down. Alexander ran up to the clearing and stopped. He was breathing hard, his face was red, and his clothes were covered in burs. He frantically looked back and forth.

"Isla, I know you're out here!" he shouted. He slowly started to walk into the meadow, watching his step and squinting through the grass. "I'm not going to hurt you. You can trust me! Just come out, and we'll talk."

Isla wanted to believe him. She didn't want to think he'd hurt her. Just yesterday, she had trusted him. She had told him more than she'd told anyone but Cash about all they'd learned and found. This was the same man who called her squirt, shared his dessert with her, let her play on his phone, took her to get milkshakes, and was best friends with her dad.

"Why are you doing this?" Isla called shakily.

Alexander froze, trying to figure out where her voice had come from. He changed direction and began walking toward her.

"You know that disc you said you found? That disc belongs to me and my business partner. He lost it while scoping out the property." He paused and peered at the grass, trying to see where Isla was. "I need ten thousand acres to build a park. Your father is the only one in the area who has that kind of land. So I hired someone to make your dad an offer. But your father wouldn't sell, and he's not even doing anything with the property. I figured a fire would scare him into selling and might even lower the value of the property. That way, I'd get it even cheaper. It's dangerous, after all, raising a kid out here. But after I had the first fire set, there was a lot of rain. Your father wasn't real shaken about the fire. He figured it was just the drought. So I decided to have my partner set another one, this time deeper into the property. That way, it would be harder to reach and would spread further."

Isla listened closely, wondering why he was telling her all of this. Was he really trusting her with this information? He was slowly headed for the middle of the meadow, but he wasn't quite going in her direction anymore. He didn't know exactly where she was. He stopped to look around before continuing.

"Listen, my partner didn't know how far I was willing to go. He thought I'd do more than I wanted to. He saw you knocked out at the bottom of a hill, so he set the fire close to you. Isla, I want you to know I had absolutely no plan of hurting you or Christopher," Alexander told her. "Now stand up, and we can talk about it more."

Isla swallowed, but she stayed put. She could see him from where she was. She didn't trust his shaking hands, his eyes—filled with anger and frustration. There was a tremor in his voice, and as he turned, something at Alexander's side caught the light. He was holding something Isla hadn't noticed until now—something that looked like a knife.

"I had absolutely no plan of hurting you or Christopher," he'd said. But now she knew, now she was onto him, it was all different. He'd ordered arson to get her father's land, and Isla had gotten caught up in all of it. Once again, Isla desperately wished she'd listened to her parents, to Cash. What wouldn't Alexander do now to stop her from telling all she knew and to succeed in his plan?

Isla's heart pounded so loud she felt sure he would hear it. She bit her tongue in an effort to keep from screaming or making any other noise. She tasted blood, hot and coppery in her mouth, and wanted to cry even as she was so scared she thought she'd be sick. Her feet throbbed and stung. Grass was sticking to their bottoms, and somewhere in the back of her mind she noted her desperate dash away from Alexander and Carlos must've messed even her toughened feet up—bad. Isla wanted to believe Alexander would never hurt her, but then why did he have a knife? She couldn't take any chances. She had to find a way to escape, and she had to do it fast. So many scenarios were racing through her head. *There's a big stick right here—maybe if I flung it at him and ran . . . or maybe if I kick him just right . . . or what if I could call the squirrels . . . or maybe—no, that's impossible . . .*

Suddenly, Isla felt a slight vibration in the ground. It seemed to be coming from beyond a hill behind the meadow, getting closer and harder beneath her. Isla gulped hard; her racing heart began to beat even faster. *The deer! It must be the deer, and there's a lot of 'em!* She wasn't even sure if they would still respond to her distressed call. She hadn't tried that in months. Before, she could cry out, and her "mother doe" would come running to protect her.

Her heart blazed as a last, desperate plan unfolded in her mind. If it actually worked, the bucks might even protect her from Alexander.

Isla prayed in her head, *Lord, I need a miracle—a miracle only you can provide.*

Alexander had been searching the meadow, carefully pushing through the grass, trying to find her and getting closer all the time. Isla swallowed hard and tried to think of the exact sound she used to make. She would have to be loud, clear, and correct. If she did it wrong, the deer would run away, and Alexander would find her. Taking a few breaths, she prepared her vocal cords.

Without warning, she let out a high-pitched scream—a scream made only by baby animals being attacked. Alexander nearly jumped out of his skin and looked right at her. Then, the ground started to shake. A loud thudding pounded over the ground.

"What did you *do*?" Alexander cried, beginning to lunge toward her.

Isla sprang up to run again and saw the most amazing thing she had ever seen. An enormous buck came flying down the hill along with a herd of at least ten deer. Isla yelled with excitement as the herd came gliding right toward her. She turned her head to see Alexander. His face had gone chalk white, and he was rigid as a board, obviously trying to choose between fight or flight. Flight quickly came over him, and he ran down the meadow.

The mighty buck flew right past Isla, along with three younger bucks. They beelined right for Alexander while the does rushed to Isla. She sobbed tears of joy and exhausted relief as a doe worriedly sniffed her. She recognized it; it was her "mother doe." Isla hugged her neck, unafraid of scaring the doe. A terrified yell rang out in the distance. Isla swung her head around. They'd got him. They were out of sight; he must have been chased into the woods. But she didn't care. She just wanted to find her way home.

Isla took off toward their old dirt road, the does following close behind. Everything seemed so surreal. Oh, how the tables had turned. Predator had become prey, and prey had become victor in a matter of seconds. The adrenaline made her feel as though she were running over a golf field instead of the brush. Her feet throbbed, and Isla knew she'd have to see what she'd done to them sooner or later, but for now, she couldn't care less. All she wanted was to get home to her dad.

As Isla neared the house, she heard sirens roaring in the distance. The does slowed down, startled by the sudden sounds, but Isla tore through the brush even harder. She was close enough to see lights. Isla grinned ear to ear; the barbed wire was only a few feet away. She dove right through the broken place in the barbed wire and somersaulted onto the dirt road. A police car came to a screeching stop just a few feet away from her.

"Dad!" she yelled at the top of her lungs.

Her eyes grew round as she looked all around. There were fire trucks, ambulances, police cars, and people everywhere. They appeared to be in the process of forming search parties, and she knew that sometime in the night or this morning, her dad must have realized she was missing. Ferdinand barked with purpose and ran toward her—it was the fastest she'd seen him move in years.

"Ferdy!" Isla yelled, falling to her knees and throwing her arms around his neck.

He wagged his tail and whimpered as he sniffed her, nosing the scrapes on her shins through her ripped jeans, the scratches on her arms from running through the brush, and her feet, which suddenly hurt so bad Isla gasped and swayed on her knees.

"Isla!" her dad shouted from among the sea of people.

He ran to her. His hair was all ruffled up, and his shirt wasn't buttoned up properly He swooped down and scooped her up. He hugged her tight, eyes glistening as if he were about to cry.

"Where were you! What happened to you?" he demanded, looking down at her bloody feet.

"Alexander," Isla said as she began to cry once more. "He did it, and he's still out there!"

Paramedics ran up with a gurney. Christopher looked into the woods as policemen with dogs began to make their way through the barbed wire. For once, he seemed to understand her perfectly, and his knuckles tightened as fear and worry gave way to rage. The paramedics took Isla from him and lifted her onto the gurney. Her dad took a step toward the woods.

"Wait, Dad, please stay with me!" Isla yelled. Turning away from the woods, he took her hand, and his face began to soften. "It's OK, Dad, the bucks got 'em," Isla muttered, laying her head back on the gurney.

"What do you mean?" he asked as they hoisted the gurney into the ambulance.

But as the crazy adrenaline of the morning passed away, Isla's pain and exhaustion were beginning to overwhelm her.

Her feet throbbed, and her head spun, and she just squeezed her dad's hand tighter, unable to explain.

"I'll tell them he might be injured," a passing policeman said as the ambulance doors closed.

The ambulance started down the road. As Isla's eyes fluttered closed, she saw glimpses of paramedics bustling and her dad praying. Soon she finally drifted into the deep sleep her body had been craving. She'd done it. It was over.

CHAPTER SEVENTEEN

Beeping . . . Why do I hear beeping? Isla thought.

She was curious and wanted to open her eyes, but she was far more exhausted than curious. Her eyelids felt as if they had weights attached to them. She tried to remember why she was so tired and sore, but she just couldn't seem to reach the memory. She took a deep breath. This place didn't smell like her room. It smelled like . . .

Isla's eyes shot open, and she groaned, "Not again." Once again, she was in the hospital. Except this time, she had no idea why.

"Isla, how do you feel?" a soft voice spoke.

Isla slowly looked around and gasped. "Mom!"

She lifted her arms up, desperate to reach her. Her mom sat on the edge of the bed and hugged her. Isla clung to her, afraid her mom would disappear if she let go. Without even realizing it, she'd begun to cry. After a moment, she released her grip and looked into her mom's eyes. It was so good to see her, but her eyes were watering too. She gently moved Isla's hair off of her face.

"Is it really you?" Isla asked.

Her mom smiled. "Yes, it's me." Isla looked across the room to see her dad was there too.

She looked at her parents, confused. "Why are we here? What happened?"

She tried to move her legs but found it was very difficult. Looking down at her feet, her eyes opened wide. They were thoroughly bandaged, and she couldn't feel her feet or most of her legs.

"What happened?" Isla asked, this time a little frantically. "Are my feet even there?"

"Your feet will be fine," her dad assured her. "You have stitches, but the doctors expect them to heal perfectly."

"Stitches! Why did I need stitches?" she asked, looking back and forth at her parents.

Her dad gently spoke. "You tried to catch the arsonists all on your own. Remember?"

Isla thought for a moment. Then it all slowly started coming back to her.

"Alexander," she said grimly. "He did it. He set the fires." A lump formed in her throat, and she dashed another tear from angry eyes.

"I know," her dad said softly, sounding a little choked up. "When I think of what he might have done to you—" His eyebrows furrowed, and he began to tense up. Isla's mom reached out and grabbed his hand. He relaxed then, just a little.

He sat on the edge of the bed with Isla's mother. "I really wish you hadn't gone after him. It was awful brave, but you could have gotten seriously hurt or even killed. In fact, going after the arsonist yourself almost cost you your right foot. You really scared us, Isla."

Isla looked down. "You're right. It was dumb. I knew that as soon as I saw 'em pull up. But they were burning down our land! I just had to stop 'em, and you wouldn't let me out there until they were caught. I'm sorry."

He smiled weakly. "I forgive you. We'll talk about consequences more later. Right now, we just want you home safe."

He leaned forward and hugged her. Isla gulped, holding back tears. "What do you mean, it almost cost me my foot?" she asked, looking down at her bulky bandage nervously.

"You had a real big cut on the bottom. At first, the doctors were really concerned about it. But it wasn't as severe as they originally thought. Don't worry about it; it'll heal in time," her dad said.

"What about Alexander? Is he in the hospital?" Isla asked.

Her parents exchanged glances. "Yes, he and his partner are both in the hospital. From what I've heard, Alexander hasn't said much, but the partner is singing like a bird," her dad said.

"Are they real hurt?" Isla wanted to know.

"The doctors and police say they both should recover in time. But I'd rather talk about you. How do *you* feel?" her dad asked.

Isla thought for a moment. "Sore, but not in pain."

Her mom nodded. "Good. Yeah, you're going to be sore for a few days, honey, and you'll be taking pain medicine for a little while. But I figure you'll be just fine."

"You feel good enough for a little company?" her dad asked.

"Company?" Isla asked hopefully.

"Seems you got popular while I've been gone," Isla's mom smiled. "There's a line of people waiting to see you."

"Can they come in?" Isla asked.

"I'll go get 'em," her dad told her. He left, and Isla looked up at her mom.

"When did you get here?"

"Late last night," her mom said.

"What time is it now?" Isla asked.

"It's almost noon," her mom replied. "We'll be able to leave soon. And guess what?"

"What?"

Her mom squeezed her knee. "We don't have to worry about arsonists anymore," she said, with just a touch of irony, as if she wished too that the arsonists had been caught in a slightly less exciting way.

But Isla smiled. It felt good to finally hear those words.

"How long will you stay in Texas?" she asked hesitantly. She was only now realizing how much she'd missed her mom. She didn't want her to leave again.

"I'll stay until you get better, then I'll go back to Scotland. But this time, I'm bringing Grandma Ainsley back," Isla's mom promised. "Even if I have to drag her all the way, she's just going to have to get used to living in Texas. I can't leave you and your dad again, especially if you're chasing down criminals now."

Isla blushed and grinned and leaned her head on her mom's shoulder. Then the door swung open. Cash shoved his way through and ran to Isla's bedside.

"Eager little thing, aren't ya?" her dad said with a laugh.

"Isla, I can't believe you actu—whoa!" Cash exclaimed, catching sight of her feet. "Did the guy shoot you in both feet?" Cash asked in a high-pitched voice, face full of awe and concern.

Isla laughed, "No, I accidentally did that from running."

"So what exactly happened! No one's telling me anything!" Cash said, almost yelling.

"Cashton, calm down! She's just woken up," a woman's voice spoke.

Isla looked up to see a short, slightly overweight woman with light brown hair held in a ponytail. She was wearing an old blue shirt and nice jeans that looked recently bought. In one hand she held a large plastic cup full of iced water. In the other she held a little boy's hand. The little boy had shorter blond hair than Cash's and big glasses with black rims and was wearing a green shirt that was far too big—probably his brother's—and blue jeans. He looked up at Isla shyly. His glasses made his eyes look twice their size, giving him an even younger and more adorable appearance.

"That's my mom, and that's Ryder," Cash quickly explained, eager to move on and talk about what happened.

"Slow down, Cash, there's no rush," his mom said again. "Nice to finally meet you, Isla. Cash'll talk my ears off every evening about you."

"Mom," Cash groaned, his cheeks turning a little red.

"Why don't you say hi to Isla?" his mom asked Ryder.

Ryder gave a little shrug and smiled, revealing slightly bucked teeth.

"I don't know," he mumbled shyly.

Isla smiled. His voice reminded her of how she used to talk. Isla waved at him with a smile. He waved back but then shyly buried his face into his mom's jeans.

Then Carroll and Darrel walked into the room. Isla looked at her father. He grinned and shrugged. She'd thought only Cash's family was there.

"Weren't we just here recently?" Darrell joked. "You must really like this place."

"Hi, Darrel," Isla laughed.

"Torri, you made it!" Carroll cried, seeing Isla's mom.

Torri jumped up to greet Carroll and Darrel. Isla turned her attention back to Cash. "So what do you already know?" Isla asked.

"That you went exploring *without me*, you caught the bad guys, and now you're in the hospital again," Cash said.

"Yeah, sorry about that. I just had to do something," Isla explained.

"You were out saving the property while I slept in bed!" Cash complained. "So who did it?"

"Remember Alexander, the one who bought us milkshakes? He and a business partner were behind it all."

"Alexander! You mean it was someone we actually knew?" He paused, taking it in. He stared at her. "Isla, we were alone with him in that truck! He could have hurt us!"

Isla looked down, frowning. "Yeah. I really thought we could trust him."

It hurt to talk about it. Even though Alexander hadn't been an important person in her life for very long, it still made her sad that he'd betrayed them. And for what? A theme park.

"Who was the other guy?" Cash asked.

"Some guy named Carlos. Alexander hired him to do all the dirty work," Isla explained. "He got bit by Ruckus."

"Ruckus bit him?"

"Yep, I led them to him when they chased me because I knew he'd bite one of them."

"Wow, I missed a lot," Cash said, disappointed.

"Don't worry, I'll explain the whole story in detail next time we explore. That way I can show you where it all happened," Isla promised.

Cash shook his head. "Just don't leave me out the next time you solve the mystery!" he told her. Isla laughed and assured him she wouldn't.

After everyone talked for a while, things settled down, and the room became quiet again. Darrel and Carroll eventually had to leave, Cash's mom and brother left the hospital to get something for lunch, and Isla's parents left to grab something from the cafeteria downstairs. But despite his huge appetite, Cash stayed behind with Isla, and she smiled happily at her best friend.

"So, I just have one more question," Cash said, sitting across from Isla on the bed.

"Shoot," Isla said.

"What on earth did Bill Cagney have to do with any of this?"

About the Author

Photo by BobStricklandPhotography.com

Isabella Allen grew up on a twenty-five acre property in Texas, where she still lives with her parents, older sister, younger brother, and rescue mutt, Paisley. She developed a love for animals and exploring at a very early age, but her real adventuring didn't start until she started venturing deeper into the property with her younger cousin as a teenager. Isabella was inspired by all of the amazing things they discovered and decided that one day she would take more people "through the barbed wire and on an adventure!" by writing a book. She didn't plan on writing this book until she was an adult with more writing experience, but she was greatly encouraged by a few people to start writing after telling a few stories at a new youth group. Isabella started creating the plot for this book that night and began writing it three days later.

About the Illustrator

Cynthia Meadows, a native Texan, has always had a passion for creating her own characters and inspiring the imagination of children with her art. After graduating from Rice University with a BA in Architecture, she decorated cakes and painted personal art pieces, eventually venturing into commercial art. Since moving to Dallas, she has illustrated storyboards, finished art for multiple ad agencies, painted pet portraits and murals, done faux finishing, worked with decorative concrete, and illustrated market comps and storyboards. Her own childhood inspiration began with *Winnie the Pooh* and *The Wind in the Willows*, and Cynthia's children's book illustrations will hopefully bring this same love of books to children and expand their world in a positive, loving way.